Books by Michael Lister

(John Jordan Novels)
Power in the Blood
Blood of the Lamb
Flesh and Blood
The Body and the Blood
Blood Sacrifice
Rivers to Blood
Innocent Blood
Blood Money
Blood Moon

(Short Story Collections)
North Florida Noir
Florida Heat Wave
Delta Blues
Another Quiet Night in Desparation

(Remington James Novels)
Double Exposure
Separation Anxiety

(Merrick McKnight Novels)
Thunder Beach
A Certain Retribution

(Jimmy "Soldier" Riley Novels)
The Big Goodbye
The Big Beyond
The Big Hello
The Big Bout

(Sam Michaels and Daniel Davis Series)
Burnt Offerings
Separation Anxiety

BLOOD MONEY
a John Jordan Mystery

by Michael Lister

Pulpwood Press
Panama City, FL

Inquiries should be addressed to:
Pulpwood Press
P.O. Box 35038
Panama City, FL 32412

Lister, Michael.
Blood Money / Michael
Lister.
-----1st ed.
p. cm.

ISBN: 978-1-888146-53-0   Hardcover

ISBN: 978-1-888146-54-7   Paperback

Book Design by Adam Ake

Printed in the United States

1 3 5 7 9 10 8 6 4 2

First Edition

For Jill Mueller

Truly an angel, and a kind, wise soul.

You have been a gift to me since the moment we began working together, a true partner in wordwork, a light that shines across oceans.

Thank You

Dawn Lister, Jill Mueller, Lou Columbus,
Mike Harrison, Dayton Lister, Phillip Weeks,
Michael Connelly, Adam Ake, Travis Roberson, Jeff Moore, Aaron Bearden, Dave Lloyd,
Dan Finley, Charlene Childers.

Chapter One

I was happy.

I had been happy before but nothing like this.

Never anything remotely resembling this.

Moments, glimpses, flashes, always fleeting, always evanescent, always tinged and diluted before had become something altogether different, something absolute, something abiding.

Of course there was much to be unhappy about—both in the macrocosm of the wide world where the wounded, stunted, and sociopathic wanted war and control and more of everything, and the microcosm of my own small world where my dad and I were about to lose our jobs, my mom was about to lose her life, and Anna's soon-to-be ex was spreading his misery around like a contact contagion—but Anna and I were together, a grace that not only made me beyond happy but put everything else into perspective.

It was a beautiful mid-September evening, a little after four—several hours before the first body would be discovered and then stolen—and Dad and I were riding out to Potter Farm for a quarterly men-only social gathering of not inconsequential political import.

I wasn't happy about that.

Being away from Anna at a social and political event with only the male movers and shakers—and wannabe movers and shakers—of Potter County and our part of the Panhandle was a special kind of hell for someone like me.

I had never been part of the good ol' boy club grasping for power and greasing of deals. The truth was I despised it. No matter how mannerly, no matter how seemingly good-natured and benign, the Old South oligarchy was not just corrupt and counter to democracy, but sexist, racist, greedy, and oppressive—a more invisible and insidious incarnation of Jim Crow.

But Dad was up for reelection and facing a very real threat in the general election after narrowly winning the primary, and it'd be political suicide for him not to attend with his supportive sons in tow.

Potter Farm was a forty-acre spread some five miles outside of town and a mile and a half from the prison, with a small lake, a barn, and a rustic old farmhouse.

Vehicles, mostly large luxury trucks, were parked on either side of the winding dirt road that led into the place—and three and four deep in the pasture beyond them.

The setting sun was mostly an orange-and-purple aura behind the farmhouse and barn and the cypress trees lining the lake, its muted glow magical, beautiful, peaceful.

Between the old house and the barn, which was set some fifty yards beyond it, large event tents had been erected beneath banks of generator-powered halogen lights.

As we searched for a place to park, Dad said, "Anything you can do to help me . . ."

I nodded.

"I know this isn't exactly your kind of . . . but . . ."

"I'll do what I can."

"What the hell?" Dad said.

I turned to see what had caught his attention.

Hugh Glenn.

"Son of a bitch's got some balls," Dad added.

Hugh Glenn was the Democratic candidate running against Dad, and though this gathering was open to the public, it was being paid for by the Republican Party of Potter County and the four candidates standing for election—Dad for sheriff, Richard Cox for judge, Don Stockton for county commissioner, and Ralph Long for property appraiser.

It was bad form for Hugh to be here, and I wondered if those running against the other three candidates were too.

By the time we parked and were climbing down out of Dad's shiny new GMC truck, Hugh Glenn had disappeared into the crowd, but Jake walked out to meet us.

"John," he said.

"Jake," I said.

Jake and I, like Cain and Abel, were brothers.

"How are you?" he asked. "You been able to stop smiling yet?"

I smiled at that and shook my head. "Not yet."

He was talking about Anna and how happy I was to finally be with her. It was said with more warmth and genuine friendliness that I was accustomed to from Jake—something he had replaced his open hostility for me with since I had helped him out of a jam or two a few weeks back.

"Good crowd," Dad said.

"Is," Jake said. "Good sign."

"Maybe. More likely they're here for the free food and booze."

Jake had been here for a while—setting up, cleaning, cooking—and not just because this was his crowd, his friends, but because as a deputy and Dad's son, his livelihood depended on Dad winning too.

"Fuckin' Hugh Glenn is here," Jake said.

"Saw him."

"And there's a lot of drinking already goin' on. I's you, I'd make the rounds, shake the hands, eat the food, make your speech, then leave before it gets late. No way the after-party ain't gettin' out of hand."

Dad nodded. "Here to do a job. Will leave as soon as it's done."

"Well, then," Jake said, "let's get to it."

Chapter Two

Later, I would think back on every interaction, every observation, attempting to recall every encounter and the thoughts and reactions they elicited, but as I moved through the throng of white men in pressed jeans, Roper Apache boots, and Brushpopper button downs, I had no way of knowing one among them would commit murder later in the night.

The first man I encountered was the head of the Potter County Republican Party, Felix Maxwell.

A largish, colorless man with gray hair and glasses, he had become the head of the party after failing several times to secure a seat in public office—either by election or appointment. He wasn't particular.

"John Jordan," he said as he squeezed and pumped my hand. "How the hell are you ol' son? Whatta you think your dad's chances are? Pretty good, huh? He could stand to be a little more social, little more friendly, but . . . I'm glad you're here with him. Means a lot to us."

"How'd this liberal get in?" someone said as he came up behind me and patted me on the back.

I turned to see Ralph Long smiling at me.

We had been friends in high school but had rarely seen each other since.

He was tall and slim with a bit of a potbelly, in khaki

slacks and a navy sport shirt with his name and *property appraiser* embroidered on it.

"No way he's a registered Republican," he said to Felix.

"Actually, ironically, I am," I said. "Had to switch from Independent to Republican to vote for Dad in the primary."

"And your good old friend and great property appraiser Ralph Long," he said.

"I started to, I really did, but then a little voice that sounded like him said he wouldn't want some old bleeding-heart convict-minister voting for him."

He laughed. So did Felix.

"How are you, man?" he said.

"Good. You?"

"Great. Never been better. It's good to see you."

"You too," I said.

"You were just kidding, weren't you?" he said. "I need every vote I can get."

I nodded. "I filled in the little circle beside your name."

"Thanks man. Please do it again in the general election."

"Plan to."

Felix said, "You let me know if there's anything I can do to convince you to stay registered for the right side."

And with that they were both gone, on to greet their several other best friends.

I looked around.

In between the two large event tents, an open bar had been set up. Small farm tractors on either side of it held iced-down bottled water and canned soft drinks in their upturned buckets.

I walked toward the tractor on the left in search of a Cherry Dr. Pepper.

On the back side of the house, several enormous charcoal grills on trailers were filled with the best steaks the Potter County Republican party could afford, the smell from them carried by the smoke wafting through the evening air making me salivate.

Negotiating my way through the swarms of men, many with drinks and cigars in their hands, was challenging—particularly while attempting to smile and nod at each one and shake the hand of more than a few.

It would be a while before the steaks and baked potatoes were served, but folding tables with white table clothes held hearty appetizers of fried catfish, oysters on the half shell, venison link sausage, and peel-and-eat boiled shrimp.

The smell of it all made me hungry and I realized I had forgotten to eat lunch. Stopping by one of the tables on my way to the bar, I tossed a couple of catfish filets on a paper plate and kept moving.

I had only taken a few steps when I saw the warden walking directly toward me.

Bat Matson, Potter Correctional Institution's new warden, had been the warden of the Louisiana State Penitentiary at Angola, the largest maximum-security prison in the country, just a few months ago.

Known as "the farm," Angola was named after the home of African slaves who used to work its plantation. The site of a prison since the end of the Civil War, Angola's eighteen thousand acres houses over five thousand men, three-quarters of whom are black, 85 percent of whom will die within its fences.

A fleshy man in his early sixties with prominent jowls and thick gray hair swooped to one side, Matson had come to Florida and to PCI with the new secretary of the department, who had been appointed by the new governor. He was authoritative, totalitarian, and fundamentalist, and not in any way fond of me.

I turned to my left to avoid him and came face to face with Anna's soon-to-be ex-husband Chris Taunton.

"Just the man I've been wanting to see," he said. "You been duckin' me?"

I reached back and dropped the plate of catfish in the large plastic garbage can behind me and turned to face him, bracing for anything he might do.

"What can I do for you, Chris?"

"Well, for starters, John, you could stop fuckin' my wife," he said.

His breath smelled strongly of whiskey, but I wasn't sure if that or his desire to embarrass me was behind his excessive volume.

Several of the men in our vicinity turned toward us.

"Your marriage being over has nothing to do with me," I said, "but it is over. I know you regret your affairs and other desperate acts and not treating that amazing woman like she deserves. Just make sure you direct that anger and disappointment in the right direction."

"Who the fuck do you think you're talkin' to?" he said.

"Chris," I said, "you've made some mistakes. Don't make others. Stop calling. Stop riding by the house. Stop—"

"It's not a house," he said. "It's a fuckin' old tin box. You're trailer trash. You're—"

"Stop the harassment. Stop making everything more difficult than it has to be."

Clinching his fists at his sides and bowing out his chest, he took another step toward me.

"You don't want to do this here," I said.

"That's where you're wrong, you self-righteous piece of shit."

Just before he took a swing, Don Stockton, the forty-something corrupt county commissioner, stepped between us and put his arms around Chris.

"This is not the place," he said. "Not the time. Come on, let's go out to my truck. There's somethin' I wanna show you."

Chris seemed to be thinking about it.

"Come on," Stockton said again. "I promise you'll like it. It'll take your mind off all this bullshit. John's not goin' anywhere. If you still want words with him later, y'all can go behind the barn when the place clears out. Okay?"

Chris shrugged Stockton's hands off but didn't make a move toward me.

"It's me," Stockton said. "You know if I say I've got something good for you then I do. Come on."

"Okay," Chris said, "but when he runs like the little pussy he is, you have to promise me you'll help me catch him."

"I promise."

"What's goin' on here, Chaplain?" Bat Matson said as he stepped up beside me.

"I'll tell you," Chris said. "Your chaplain's fuckin' a married woman. That's what."

Matson looked at me with contempt, shook his head, and kept walking.

He had only gone a short distance when he turned back and said, "My office. First thing in the morning."

When I finally reached the bar area, I found Hugh Glenn sloshing his vodka and cranberry as he spouted his qualifications and vision for the sheriff's department.

There were several men around him but only because they were in line for the bar. Still, he spoke with the conviction that his captive audience was there for him.

After I found an ice-cold Dr. Pepper in the tractor bucket, I got in the bar line for some grenadine.

"Here's Jack Jordan's secret weapon right here," Glenn said.

A few of the men turned and looked at me.

"John, what is your unofficial role in your dad's department?"

"I have no role. Unofficial or otherwise."

"How many cases do you solve for him each year?" he asked. "What percentage?"

I didn't respond.

"First thing I'm gonna do when I'm sheriff is offer you a job," he said. "How would you like to be my lead investigator?"

I still didn't respond.

"I'm serious," he said.

"Did you have anything to do with that meth lab bust last night?" a youngish strawberry-blond-haired guy I only vaguely recognized said.

I shook my head.

"Notice how drug busts go up right before an election?" Glenn said.

"You have to admit that's true," the young guy said to me.

"It's bullshit," another guy said.

He was a short, dark-haired, dark-complected guy in his late twenties.

"Don't listen to him," the guy in line behind him said to me. "His sister was one of the ones that got busted."

"Stepsister," the dark guy corrected. "Got nothin' to do with it. I'm glad her sorry ass is in jail, but if the sheriff was doin' his damn job, her loser boyfriend would've been in there years ago and last night never would've happened."

Thankfully, I reached the front of the line, got my grenadine, and was able to slip away.

"You guys enjoy your evening," I said.

I found Jake over near the barn helping fry the fish and boil the shrimp.

He was standing in front of a large outdoor deep fryer hooked to a propane bottle, stirring the boiling shrimp with a wooden boat paddle.

He wore an apron with an American flag and the words HOME OF THE FREE BECAUSE OF THE BRAVE written on it. Beneath the words was the silhouette of soldiers before a red, white, and blue background.

"Last batch," he said. "Want some fresh, hot shrimp?"

"Thanks," I said, not wanting to reject any offer of civility he made toward me and searching desperately for something to do.

"Coming up."

I thought about how much I had always loved fresh Gulf shrimp, and how the Deepwater Horizon oil spill had changed that for me. I couldn't eat anything from the Gulf without thinking of and even sometimes tasting 4.9 million barrels of oil and 1.84 million gallons of Corexit dispersant in every bite—all of which still remained under the surface of the beautiful blue-green waters, and would continue to long after we who were doing so much damage were dead and gone.

"I can take over if you want to go mingle," I said.

"Mingle?"

"What would you call it?"

"Not something gay like *mingle*," he said. "Thanks, but I'm done after this. I'll go get my mingle on then."

He knew how much using *gay* as a pejorative bothered me, but seemed to be saying it more out of habit than aggression.

Given the fragile nature of our new relationship, I let it go.

"How are the Jordan boys tonight?" Judge Richard Cox said as he walked up.

Richard Cox was a tall, trim man in his early sixties with bright blue eyes and a calm, confident manner.

He had been a judge in the county for as long as I could remember. He was respected and liked, but lacked the warmth and personableness to be loved. To the right of the most rightwing conservative, he was rigidly religious and punitive in his sentencing, but his approach to the law and life emanated from genuine conviction and he applied his judgements both in and out of the courtroom with equal severity for all.

"Just fine, Judge Cox," Jake said. "How are you?"

"Be better if I could trouble you for a few of those fresh shrimp."

"You got it."

"They've run out over there and I didn't get to try any. They're my favorite. 'Specially in that spicy cajun seasoning."

"Have all you like, Judge. We got plenty."

"Don't want any more than my fair share."

"Yes, sir," Jake said. "Of course, sir."

"Chaplain Jordan, how are you?" he said.

He said *chaplain* the way he always said it—with a hint of ironic derision. He had told me on more than one occasion that my belief in grace and the absolute unconditional love of God was misguided and dangerous, and that what he called my cheap grace, social gospel, works theology was leading weak and vulnerable people astray, away from instead of unto God.

"Good," I said. "How are you?"

"Blessed," he said. "You read any of the books I recommended to you yet?"

I shook my head.

I'd read books like them before, both in my youth and in seminary, and had no desire to ever read any like them again. They were all judgement-filled Fundamentalist rhetoric that took a literalist, exclusive approach to sacred texts and religion and were antithetical to everything Jesus taught, lived, and died for.

Dressed far more formally than anyone else in attendance, he wore a gray suit, white shirt, and black wingtips. His only concession to the casualness of the setting and event was to unbutton his top button and loosen his tie ever so slightly. His idea of letting loose.

One of his lapels held an American flag pin, the other a white button with the silhouettes of a man and a woman, an *equals* sign, and the word *marriage*.

"Well, if you boys'll excuse me, I think I'll take these shrimp to go," he said. "Have a lot of people to see and a speech to prepare for and pray about."

Each of the four candidates would have five minutes to address the crowd tonight after the pledge and prayer and before the meal.

"You think Dad is praying about his speech?" Jake asked when he was sure Cox was far enough away not to hear.

I smiled.

"He asked me to do it," I said.

"Have you?"

I shook my head. "Not yet."

"The hell you waitin' on?"

Chapter Three

The speeches were what you'd expect.

They took place on a makeshift stage consisting of a flatbed trailer that had been towed here for just that purpose. In addition to the speakers, the yellow lowboy trailer held the American and Florida flags, a Republican Party of Potter County banner, a mic on a stand, and a PA speaker on each end.

Each candidate was truly honored to serve God and the best county in the best state in the best country in the world. Their doors were always open. Small government. Answerable to the people. Washington was bad, bad, bad. Local was where it was at. Honesty. Integrity. Humility.

In the sea of white faces, I saw two black ones. One belonged to the county commissioner from the "black" district, the other, an activist minister and the pastor of the largest African-American church in Potter County.

Dad didn't do a bad job, but public speaking wasn't where he excelled.

After each candidate spoke and the host and the organizer and the head of the party recognized and thanked everyone several times and took the opportunity to promote themselves and their projects and agendas, dinner was served at a little after five.

Large, tender, juicy steaks, baked potatoes, a salad, and a roll.

The rest of the evening consisted of excessive eating, drinking, and talking—and me regretting not having driven myself.

The night wore on.

Eventually a few of the overly full, inebriated men began to stumble to their trucks and take their leave, most of them far too under the influence to drive but driving anyway.

I missed Anna. Ached for her.

But there were still voters present and Dad showed no sign of stopping until he had spoken to everyone individually.

As I scanned the still not insubstantial crowd for someone to talk to, I saw only one face that looked even more miserable than I felt.

Richard Cox, Jr. was sitting at one of the tables in the corner of the event tent alone, nursing what looked to be a Tom Collins.

I found him staring blankly into the bottom of his glass.

"Richie, if you're contemplating suicide just remember they'll run out of food and booze eventually," I said as I walked up to stand across the table from him.

"John, I didn't know you were here. How are you?"

"Been better," I said, indicating the event.

"I'm being punished for my sins," he said.

I smiled.

"I'm truly shocked he even wants me here."

Though not out, there was no doubt about Richie's sexual orientation—something that must keep his homophobic dad up nights.

He was a talented actor and theater director, frustrated by the few opportunities the Panhandle offered him.

"Pretty sure the demographic I appeal to isn't here," he added. "Though I did see one or two public servants I've serviced before."

"If my dad's one of 'em don't tell me," I said.

"Honey, you can smell the straight on him."

"Actually, it's Old Spice," I said, "but I can see why you'd confuse the two."

He laughed.

"Your dad's all right," he said. "Mine's the prick."

I started to say something but Richard Cox, Sr. called to him from across the way.

"Richie, come over here. There's someone I want you to meet."

"Duty calls," he said, rising wearily and a bit unsteadily. "By the way, when you gonna let me write and direct a play about your life?"

He had asked before and like before I just laughed it off.

Walking beside him for several steps to make sure he was okay, I broke off and wandered down in the direction of the lake, passing the barn, leaving the pandering and promise-making behind.

The moon was just a small silver sliver in a cloud-tinged sky, but was enough to shimmer on the glass surface of the lake.

The air was damp and cool and the dew on the ground caused sand and small blades of grass to cling to my shoes as I followed the slope down to the water's edge.

As I neared the closest bank, I became aware of a figure leaning against a pond pine, the red glow of a cigarette tip blazing in the dark.

"Showin' any sign of stopping?" she asked.

"The shindig?" I said, nodding. "Food and booze are nearly all gone. Won't be long now. You waiting for someone?"

"Sort of," she said. "Waiting for this farce to end so the real party can begin. You stayin' for it?"

It was dark. Her disembodied voice all there was of her save for red lips, pale skin, and blond hair seen intermittently in the red glow accompanying big, long drags.

"It?"

"The after-party. You're cute. You should stay. There's poker, real liquor, cigars, and me."

"You're . . ."

"The entertainment," she said. "Won't be the only one. There'll be others if I'm not your type."

"Only have one type," I said. "And she's waiting at home for me."

"Ah, that's so sweet. Is it true?"

"As true as anything you'll ever hear."

"Well, damnation honey, a simple yes would've sufficed."

I smiled, but shook my head. "No. It really wouldn't've."

"Gotcha handsome," she said. "You're a one-woman man and you don't care who knows it. Not many of those left these days. And I'm in a position to know."

"Hey John," Richie yelled. "You down there?"

He was standing near the barn, backlit by the bank of halogen lights.

"Yeah."

"I talked my sister into comin' to pick me up. You wanna ride?"

"There's your big chance to get home to your one-

and-only type," she said. "You gonna take it?"

"Thanks," I yelled back to Richie. "I'll be right there."

"There's a shocker," she said.

"Can we give you a lift somewhere?" I asked.

"Have you been listening, sugar?"

"I have," I said, "which is why I'm offering you a ride out of here."

"Whatta you know," she said, "an honest to God good Joe. Thanks, but I got work to do."

I took out one of my cards and handed it to her.

"You change your mind," I said, "just give me a call. I'll come back out and get you."

She shined the light from her cellphone onto the card.

In the spill and reflection from the light, I could see that she was a shortish, thickish, heavily made-up blonde with large breasts dressed and like a TV prostitute.

"Prison chaplain?" she said. "No shit?"

"None."

"Okay, Chap," she said. "I'll call you if I need you."

Chapter Four

"**N**o women allowed," Diane Cox was saying. "Why? It's so creepy."

"You're preaching to the choir, sister," I said.

"Do they do secret man stuff? Walk around, dicks swinging, drinking testosterone and plotting how to oppress women even more?"

"You know Dad wouldn't be party to that," Richie said. "Well, at least the dicks swinging part. His might touch another man's and he'd go straight to hell."

"The shit we do for our dads," I said.

"You have a reputation, you know," Diane said to me. "I've heard about you. Really surprises me you'd be at something like that."

"See previous answer," I said. "Being a dutiful son."

"How far does that go?"

"That far," I said. "That was the limit."

"Thanks for gettin' us out of there, Dir," Richie said.

"I did it for our father as much as you," she said. "Knew it was only a matter of time until you had enough to drink and did or said something that would cost him the election."

"Would that be so bad?"

"Far worse than you think," she said. "Try living this

year without his . . . ah . . . assistance, and let me know how that works out for you."

"Dir?" I asked.

"Huh?"

"You called her Dir."

"Oh. Started as Dirty Diana back when the song came out. Then Dirty and eventually Dir."

"It true you're beddin' Anna Rodden?" Diane asked.

"Dir," Richie scolded.

"What?"

"They haven't invented a word for what we're doing," I said, "but beddin' doesn't even begin it."

"Oh my," she said. "A romantic."

"And then some," Richie said.

"Lucky girl," she said.

"I'm the lucky one."

"That you think that makes her a very lucky girl."

Dirty Diana thinks you're a very lucky girl to be bedded by me," I said.

I found Anna asleep on the couch, braless in a soft T-shirt and yoga pants, one of my old theology books resting on her breasts.

"I am," she said.

She slid over toward the back cushions and I sat down next to her, hugging and kissing her as I did.

"I missed you," I said.

"Was it torturous?"

I nodded. "Pretty damn bad."

"Who's Dirty Diana? Thought no women were allowed."

"Judge Cox's daughter. She picked up Richie and

they gave me a ride."

"I hope she said it in front of him. Me not even divorced yet and pregnant with another man's child. It'd give him conniptions."

"Still wouldn't be as bad as if you were a dude," I said, "but sadly, no. She didn't say it in front of him."

"How does she know we're beddin' one another?"

"Apparently, everyone does."

"What'd you tell her?"

"That I was the lucky one."

"Such a good, sweet man. I'm the luckiest girl in the whole wide world."

"Do you know how long I've waited to be with you?" I asked.

"I do. Same as I've waited to be with you. Forever."

I touched her cheek.

"Sorry about this place," I said, looking around at my old trailer. "Didn't realize just how bad it had gotten until you moved in."

"There's nowhere else on earth I'd rather be."

"We'll find a place soon."

"No rush. Really. I've never been happier anywhere."

"We'll look some more after work tomorrow."

I was sleeping very soundly when the call came. And dreaming.

I was dreaming of being trapped in an airplane submerged in the sea. I was trying to make my way up to where Anna was, but the people between us were panicking and the floating debris was so thick, I couldn't get to her.

I startled awake, my heart pounding, but began to settle down the moment I reached over and felt Anna there in the bed beside me, her skin smooth and warm.

"Hello."

"Chaplain?"

"Yeah?"

"It's Sergeant Sterzoy from the control room. Sorry to wake you, sir, but we've got a . . . we've got something . . . a situation. I know the warden wouldn't want me to call you so please don't let him know I did, but . . ."

"I won't," I said. "What is it?"

"A young woman," he said. "Trying to break in to the prison. Well, I mean she was. She's . . . she's dead now."

"Trying to break in?" I said. "Is that how she got killed?"

"No, sir. We found her that way. She was already dead. And your card was in her pocket."

"I'm on my way."

Chapter Five

As I drove to the institution, I thought about who the victim could be and why she would be trying to break in to the prison.

I gave a lot of my cards out—especially to the families of inmates. Was it one of them trying to get in to see their boyfriend or husband or son? Probably not the last, since Sterzoy called her a *young woman*, but I couldn't rule it out.

My phone rang again as I neared the institution. It was Dad.

"Sorry to call so late but we've got a situation at the prison," he said. "Can you meet me out here?"

"I'm pulling up now."

I parked in the mostly empty lot in front of the admin building, and when I rounded the corner in front of the main gate and control room, Dad was waiting for me.

"Who called you?" Dad asked.

"As far as the warden knows, you did," I said.

He nodded.

I got into his truck and we rode around the perimeter of the prison toward the flashing lights flickering in the darkness in the distance.

The entire prison was surrounded by an asphalt road used by a roving perimeter patrol. We were driving on it down the east side of the institution.

When we reached the scene, Dad pulled up at an angle and shined his lights on the area, adding them to the deputy's car and prison patrol vehicle already doing the same.

Though the light was uneven and dim and the deputy's flashers hindered instead of helped visibility, they provided enough illumination to show a white woman in her midtwenties standing stiffly in front of the fence, her body leaning forward at an odd angle, only her face actually touching the chain link.

I could see well enough to identify the victim and determine she had been placed here after she died.

"Chaplain, Sheriff," Officer Barber said by way of greeting.

He was a young CO with puffy, acne-scarred cheeks and a brown buzz cut. His brown uniform hung loosely on his narrow frame.

The night was cooler than before, a brisk breeze biting at our faces and waving ever so slightly the chain link and razor wire.

"Any idea who she is or how she got here?" Dad asked.

"No sir. I was makin' my rounds and there she was. I had passed by no more than twenty minutes before and she wasn't there. She was just standing there. Leaning really, I guess. Not moving. I radioed the control room. I was surprised her touching the fence didn't alert them already anyway."

"And she was just like this?" Dad said. "Hasn't moved?"

"Hasn't moved so much as a millimeter. The only thing I've done was feel for a pulse and search her for identification. All she had was the chaplain's card, a couple of condoms, and four hundred-dollar bills in that little purse across her shoulder."

The prison was situated on hundreds of acres of clear, open land. It extended behind us for some two hundred yards to a pine tree forest, a mile or so beyond which was Potter Farm.

The silver sliver of moon was higher now, its faint, fog-muted beam still streaking the charcoal sky.

Dad turned to me. "You recognize her?"

I nodded. "She was at Potter Farm tonight," I said. "Down by the lake, waiting for the political part of the party to end and the crowd to scatter. Said she was there for the after-party."

Dad shook his head. "God almighty. That's all we need."

"I have no idea who she is," I said. "I just spoke to her briefly. Offered her a ride and gave her my card in case she got into anything out there she needed help with."

"It's almost as if she was trying to climb in to get to you," Barber said.

Dad looked at the deputy, who had yet to say a word. "Where's Jake?"

"Still at the farm, as far as I know."

Dad shook his head.

"Was playing poker the last time I saw him," the deputy added.

"Them and that goddamn after-party," Dad said. "Gonna cost me the goddamn election. Radio and tell him to keep everybody there and you go help him do just that. I'll be over there just as soon as I can."

The deputy left—and with him part of the illumination and all of the annoying blue strobing.

"I called FDLE as soon as I got word," Dad said.

"Crime scene unit should be here within the hour."

I nodded.

"Warden and inspector are on their way," Barber said.

Dad and I stepped closer to the young woman.

She had on the same TV prostitute clothes that I had glimpsed her in earlier in the evening—a shimmering sequined top with spaghetti straps, a bottom of the butt-cheeks bedazzled blue jeans skirt, and candy-apple-red peep-toe pumps.

Her body was stiff with rigor and showed signs of fixed lividity from where it had lain after she was killed but before she was moved.

Her pose was both creepy and surreal, standing death-still with her head against the fence like a devotee praying at the wailing wall.

Kneeling down on the ground beside her and looking up, I could see the wounds, the cuts and scrapes and bruises, of her bloodied face. Given those and the general swelling of her misshapen head, I'd guess she was beaten to death, her unnatural and untimely demise caused by blunt force trauma.

"Somebody beat the living shit out of her," Dad said.

I nodded.

"Why bring her here?" he said. "She couldn't've made it on her own, could she?"

I shook my head. "She was moved after she died."

"Why here?"

"Potter Farm is right through there," I said, pointing to the woods beyond the field behind us.

The warden's car screeched to a stop on the road behind Dad's truck, and Bat Matson and the institutional inspector jumped out.

Matson's fleshy face was red and even more puffy than usual, his jowls bobbing as he bounced in our direction. Instead of swooping to the side, his thick gray hair stood on end, waving in the wind.

"Just what in the hell is goin' on here?" he said. "And why is the warden the last one to arrive at a crime scene in his prison?"

Barber tried to explain and placate as best he could, but Matson would have none of it.

"And just what the hell is the chaplain doing here? You're not needed. I have no idea why you're here, unless you're disobeying a direct order of mine, but you need to go home. Be in my office first thing in the morning."

"Whoa now," Dad said. "Wait just a damn minute. He's here as a witness. Not a chaplain. His card was the only thing found on the victim. He spoke to her earlier tonight."

"But—"

"He's here because the chief law enforcement officer of the county asked him to be."

"I don't like this, not one bit," Matson said. "I'm in charge of my own damn institution, by God."

"Nobody said you weren't, but this is a murder investigation and I'm in charge of it."

"Actually, *Sheriff,* the IG of the Department of Corrections is in charge of all investigations at the institutions."

"I've worked with the IG several times before," Dad said, "and have no problem when he's the lead investigator when he has jurisdiction, but jurisdiction is established by where the crime took place, not where the body is found. She was clearly killed somewhere else and placed here. I have jurisdiction and this is my investigation. Understand?"

Matson took a moment to settle himself down a bit.

"Very well then," he said. "Okay, what have we got?"

Dad told him—with a little help from Barber.

The interim institutional inspector, Mark Lawson, a thick, heavily tattooed twenty-six-year-old who was little more than Matson's puppet, never uttered a word.

"So we have no idea who she is or why she's leaning against my fence?"

"Not yet. But we will. And soon too. As soon as FDLE gets here and we process the scene, we're going to interview the last people to see her alive."

"*We?*" Matson said beneath raised eyebrows and challenging eyes.

"Yes," Dad said. "My department."

"Do you have any idea why the killer would bring her here or pose her body like that?" Dad asked me.

We were standing back from the scene a bit, just the two of us, waiting on FDLE to arrive. Matson was down the way busy calling the inspector general and the secretary of the department to report what had happened. The institutional inspector was busy watching.

Mention of the IG inevitably led to thoughts of my ex-father-in-law, Tom Daniels, and his daughter, my ex-wife Susan, and the unfinished business I still had with both of them.

"I honestly can't come up with anything," I said.

"Is it random or does it carry some kind of significance for the killer?" he said.

"No way to know," I said. "But since it's not apparent to us, if it does have meaning it must be only to him."

"She had to meet whoever killed her at our party," he said.

"Most likely."

He shook his head slowly.

We were quiet a moment, which only pronounced Matson's conversation and amplified his voice.

"Wonder if it's political?" Dad said. "Meant to embarrass me and make me lose the election."

It was as irrational as it was extreme, and it reminded me of the blind spot and touch of paranoia he had when it came to politics in general and his job in particular.

I shook my head. "Guess we can't rule it out, but I can't imagine anyone doing something so extreme given the stakes and situation."

"Well, it's what's going to happen whether it was intended or not."

"Maybe we can prevent that from happening," I said.

We fell silent again and this time there was only the sad, lonely sound of the wind.

Finally, FDLE arrived and began to process the scene.

There wasn't much to it so it didn't take long.

When they were finished, the lead tech, a diminutive man named Denis, came over and gave Dad a preliminary report.

"I'm sure you already know everything I'm gonna say. This wasn't where the victim was killed. The body was moved here after death. We'll come back in the morning when there's light, but so far we've found nothing—no usable footprints or tire tracks."

"When you do come back," Dad said, "let's expand the search for evidence to include this field and the woods over there. We have reason to believe the killer may have come through there. Coordinate with my office and I'll provide some deputies to help with the search."

"Will do. Sorry I don't have more for you . . ."

Robin Rouse walked up and joined our little group as Kent Clark Funeral Home loaded the body into the back of a hearse to take it to the ME's office in Panama City to await an autopsy.

Robin, a tall, thin, midforties African-American woman with short, thick black hair and a smallish head, was an investigator with the medical examiner's office. She spoke very softly and we all leaned in as she talked.

"Can't tell you much until the autopsy is complete," she said. "And anything I say is subject to change . . . but I'd say the victim died of blunt force trauma to the head. She was dead a while before her body was moved here. Rigor mortis had set in, which is how she was able to be propped up against the fence the way she was. Fixed lividity shows the victim lay on her back for a while after she was murdered and before being transported here."

"Any idea how long she's been dead?" Dad asked.

Robin shook her small head. "I could only guess."

"Would you?"

"For the body to be stiff enough to be propped up against the fence like that, rigor mortis has to be set in. In normal conditions that can take up to twelve hours. Certain things can speed it up or slow it down."

I looked at the clock on my phone. It was nearly six.

"I saw her at a little before nine," I said.

"So then it was probably sped up by heat, exertion, or drugs," she said, "but I'd still guess it happened pretty soon after you saw her."

"If she ran from her killer," I said, "and fought with him . . ."

"Then rigor would set in sooner," Robin said, "and the body would be stiff enough to prop against the fence."

Chapter Six

The first hints of dawn showed at the edges of the horizon in a nearly imperceptible softening of the darkness.

Potter Farm looked to be sleeping it off.

Trash strewn about.

Beer cans. Whiskey bottles. Paper plates.

Everything abandoned.

Empty white event tents. White plastic tables and chairs, some overturned, no one sitting, no one eating, no one present. The party over.

Every surface cold and wet from the night dew.

A handful of cars scattered throughout the large pastures where a few hours before there had been hundreds.

The thick, damp air still tinged with the smell of smoke and charcoal and grilled meat.

In the farmhouse, we found Jake, Ronald Potter, Felix Maxwell, Don Stockton, and Hugh Glenn sitting around a green felt-covered poker table, smoking cigars and playing cards.

The deputy Dad had sent over was standing awkwardly in the corner.

"You're playing with him?" Dad asked, nodding at Hugh Glenn.

"He's taking all my money," Glenn said. "Hell, I'm

now financing your campaign."

"Why didn't you want us to leave, Jack?" Don Stockton asked.

He was a corrupt county commissioner with a district so gerrymandered with family and friends, people he'd bought and bribed and traded favors with, he never had any serious threat to his seat.

"I just need to talk to y'all," Dad said. "Who else is here?"

"May be a girl or two in the rooms," Stockton said.

"Andrew, Jake, go through the rooms," Dad said. "I want everyone together in this main room right now."

Evidently the deputy's name is Andrew.

Within a few minutes, Jake and Andrew had returned with two young women who looked underage and were barely able to walk, and three more men—one old, one middle-aged, one in his thirties—all half asleep and hungover.

Both the girls and the men looked vaguely familiar, but only in the small town-bearing-a-family-resemblance kind of way.

"That everybody?"

Jake nodded.

"Who else has been here?"

"About a thousand other people, Sheriff," Felix said. "Including you. What's this all about?"

"I mean since the event ended and your little after-party began."

No one said anything.

"What time did everything outside end?" Dad asked. "What time did y'all move in here?"

"But you were here."

"Pretend I wasn't."

"I'd say around nine," Felix said. "People left pretty quick after the food and booze ran out."

"Card game started about eight-thirty," Stockton said. "There were still some people outside, but not many. They were gone by nine I'd say."

"I was one of the last to come in," Felix added. "By that time there were only a handful of people left outside and they were leaving."

"I came in right after Felix," Glenn said, looking at his phone. "It was three minutes after nine. I know because I called my wife to tell her I was going to stay. And when I came in, there was no one up around the house or barn, just a few people in the parking area, cranking up and pulling away."

"Who else has been here?" Dad said. "In here since, say, eight-thirty."

"There've been a handful or so wandering in and out," Stockton said. "Especially early on. Coach from the high school played a hand or two. So did Neil Williams and Mark Smith. Ralph Long came in for a while. Played a hand or two. Hung out. The judge decided against driving and waited in here for his daughter to come get him. Deacon Jones came in, looked around, and went out again pretty damn fast. All of 'em were gone fairly early. The warden came in and had a cigar and told us how much better Louisiana is than Florida. John's number one fan, Chris Taunton, was here. May still be. He tried to play a few hands but was too fucked up. Hell, even the high sheriff stuck his head in for a few."

"I know what I did," Dad said. "I'm asking about everyone else."

"Just answering your questions, Jack. No need to get testy."

"How'd you two get here?" Dad asked the girls.

They looked confused.

"Where's your friend?" I said.

"Who?" Stockton said. "They drove themselves. It was just them. They partied a little too hard, so I wouldn't let them drive. Was letting them sleep it off."

"Nobody saw a third girl?" I said. "Blonde. Older. Bigger. But dressed like these two."

No one had.

"I seen another girl outside," the girl to Jake's left said. "But she wasn't our friend though. And she didn't come in or nothin'."

"What'd she look like?" I asked.

"Like you said, I think. It was pretty dark."

"What was she doing?"

"I didn't pay her much mind. Nothin'. Just sort of hangin'. Like she's waitin' on somebody or somethin'."

"I think she come inside," the other girl said. "I came down to pee. She was standin' at the back door. I opened it for her. I didn't see her when I came out from peeing. Guess she could've not come in. Just figured she did."

"Who else saw her?" Dad said.

Either no one had or was willing to admit they had.

"I want statements and contact information from everyone before you leave. And tell the absolute truth. No matter what. Don't lie to us. We're gonna find the truth."

"About what?" Stockton said again. "What is this all about?"

"The young lady that John described and this young lady opened the door for was found dead not far from here."

"Now wait just a minute," Stockton said. "You should've told us that first. We didn't have anything to do with that. We're not—"

"How old are these young ladies, Don?" Dad said.

"Twenty something."

"I wanna see their driver's licenses and I want to know everybody's whereabouts and anything you can remember that went on last night, understand?"

"**E**verything was pretty much like they said," Jake was saying.

He, Dad, and I were standing outside the farmhouse, the day beginning to break around us.

Inside, Andrew and two other deputies were taking statements from everyone.

"They left shit out," he added, "but I didn't hear any outright lies."

"Did the poker game last all night?" I said.

"Yeah, but guys came and went. They'd play for a while, then go off, then come back later and be dealt back in."

"Where'd they go?" I asked.

"You know."

"Say it anyway," Dad said.

"To dip their wicks."

"Do you know how young they are?" Dad said. "You tryin' to sabotage my campaign or are you just that—"

"Did you go back there with them?" I asked.

"Just one."

"Did everybody?"

"I think so. Some a few times I think."

"Did Hugh Glenn?" Dad asked.

"Definitely."

"Were the girls drugged?" I asked.

"Fuck no. They were drinkin'. I saw one of 'em pop a pill or two, but nobody gave 'em anything."

"That you know of," I said.

"Jake," Dad said, "what the hell were you thinkin'?"

"Wasn't, I guess," he said. "But hell, I was with the head of the Republican Party and a county commissioner. Hell, all the leaders of the county had been here . . . I just thought . . ."

"You thought this group of men are untouchable," I said.

"Well, they are, aren't they?"

"Thought they do what they want."

"Well, they do, don't they?"

"Thought you were one of them," I said. "A least for a night."

He hung his head. "Guess I did. I mean I didn't. Not like that exactly, but I guess that's what it comes down to."

"No way this doesn't cost me my job," Dad said. "No way."

Before either of us could respond, his phone rang. "Sheriff Jordan."

We waited while he took the call.

Dad didn't say anything, but based on his expressions and reactions, he was receiving some shocking news.

"You're not gonna believe this," he said when he ended the call. "This night just keeps gettin' better and better. The hearse from Kent Clark carrying the victim to the morgue was forced off the road and the body was stolen at gunpoint."

"Who the hell would steal a . . ." Jake said. "And why? The fuck they want with—"

"The killer most likely," I said. "Probably thought he left something incriminating behind."

"He probably did too," Dad said. "Dammit. And now it's gone."

"I'm sure there are other reasons too," I said. "To conceal her identity . . . to . . ."

"But why display her the way he did just to steal her back a little while later?"

I thought about it. Nothing came to mind. "There had to be something—something he didn't think of until later after he staged the body the way he did, something important, urgent enough to make him risk stealing it back, but I can't think of what that would be."

"If we find him," Dad said, "we can ask him."

Before we could respond or make a move toward finding the body thief, my phone vibrated in my pocket.

I withdrew it to see that the prison was calling.

"Chaplain Jordan," I said.

"Chaplain, it's Nurse Stewart. We've had another suicide attempt. How soon can you get here?"

"I'm on my way."

Chapter Seven

The slackness in the rope pulled taut as the body dropped, his own weight tightening the noose around his neck.

He kicked his feet, searching for purchase, flung his arms about, grabbing the air. Panic filled his wide eyes, and he flailed wildly as if falling from a great height.

The short fall wasn't long enough to snap his neck and crush his spinal cord.

This wasn't a hanging. It was death by strangulation. And it wouldn't be quick.

Thoughts sped through his mind in ever increasing rapidity, while everything around him moved in slow motion.

Somebody screamed.

Time passed.

Nothing happened.

A figure in white moved outside his cell like a series of still-frame photos being casually flipped through.

The angel of death?

Come to fly him away to heaven or fling him down to hell?

He tried to inhale, but could not. The best he could do was small gasps of breath, none of which made it down to his lungs.

The figure stopped at the door of the cell, unable to

open it. Only a figure in brown would have a key.

More footsteps clanged on the metal grate of the catwalk. Maybe they signaled the approach of someone who could unlock the door of this six-by-nine concrete-and-steel coffin.

Maybe he'd survive this after all.

But as the rope bit into his flesh and the ruby-red bruise necklace appeared around his neck, he feared they would not make it in time.

Head pounding.

Pressure building.

Eyes bulging.

A serpentine trickle of blood ran from his nose, slithered across his lips, and snaked down his chin.

Can't breathe. Can't . . .

More time passed. Time he didn't have. It rushed past him like the final seconds in a midnight countdown on a death-chamber clock.

This inhumane space he occupied was no longer just figuratively unbearable.

Please, God. I don't want to die. Not here. Not like this.

More time.

More passing. His passing.

Where're the keys? What's taking so long?

Light-headed.

Sleepy.

Sleep. Perchance to dream. Ay, there's the rub. For in that sleep of death what dreams may come?

Where had that come from? What class? Which teacher? Didn't matter. Nothing did.

Maybe they didn't want to find the key fast enough. Maybe this was their idea of entertainment.

Now he couldn't breathe at all.

The light in the cell began to dim, the figure in white beyond the door fading. As he lost consciousness, his head fell forward, his purplish face quickly becoming the color of his swollen, protruding tongue.

Every thirteen minutes, someone in the United States commits suicide.

Each year in this country there are over thirty-five thousand official suicides.

Unofficially, many experts say the actual number could be three times that. Official suicide statistics are notoriously unreliable. Large numbers of suicides are never reported—often because of the lengths families will go to in order to hide the suicide of a loved one.

Avoiding the social stigma or loss of life insurance benefits, many families hide suicide as if it were daddy's empty booze bottles, mama's pain pill addiction, or daughter's eating disorder.

Other suicides occur under such ambiguous circumstances that officials attribute them to accidents rather than the willful destruction of one's own life.

Actual suicides each year are more likely upwards of ninety-thousand—with attempts at eight to ten times that.

Suicide accounts for more deaths each year than murder, and it ranks tenth among leading causes of death.

Although women attempt suicide three times more often than men, men complete suicide three times more often than women.

Suicide is self-murder. It's different from any other death because those left behind cannot direct their anger at the unfairness of a random act or the brutality of a murderer. Instead, they grieve for the very person who has taken their loved one from them.

Sometimes suicide makes a certain sense.

Sometimes it's the greatest mystery of all, more mysterious than death itself.

And sometimes it isn't suicide at all.

Chapter Eight

"**I** *didn't* try to kill myself, Chaplain," Lance Phillips said from within the Suicide Observation Status cell. "I'm not suicidal. My life's never been better."

"Statements like that undercut your credibility," I said.

"It's true."

"Do you know where you are?"

He was in an empty isolation cell in the infirmary of Potter Correctional Institution, wearing nothing but a heavy canvas shroud over his pale, thin frame. The cell was located in the medical department inside the infirmary, and it was designed to house inmates who represented a threat to themselves or others—everything from infectious disease to suicide.

"Nothing the state of Florida can come up with compares to the prison of addiction," he said.

I was seated in an uncomfortable and wobbly folding chair outside the cell, a solid metal door with two large panels of steel-reinforced glass windows separated by a food tray slot between us. We communicated through the open food slot, which we would have done even if he had been isolated because of an infectious disease. The cell was equipped with a negative air flow system.

"The nurse said you tried to hang yourself."

Lance Phillips's height didn't match his weight. He was probably three inches or so over six feet, but weighed around a hundred and thirty pounds, and his hands and feet were small and feminine. His skin was pale and so were his too-small blue eyes.

"Well, I didn't."

I glanced down at the large white bandage around his neck and he followed my gaze. He reached up and touched his throat with his small hand and caressed the bandage gently.

"I know you think I'm crazy, but don't you see? That's the beauty of it."

"Of what?"

"Killing someone and making it look like suicide. Someone like me. An inmate? Especially since . . ."

"Since what?"

"Since . . . I've attempted suicide before."

I nodded.

He was right. If someone were trying to murder him, it'd be the perfect cover. And if someone were really trying to disguise a homicide as a suicide—especially in a locked confinement cell, then that someone was a creative and cunning killer.

"See," he said, "you don't believe me."

"I don't disbelieve you," I said. "I'm just listening, taking everything in."

The tension left his face for the first time, and he pushed his light brown hair up off his forehead. "I need your help. No one else in here gives a damn—that's another reason this guy's never been caught."

"You're saying you're not the first. We've had murders made to look like suicides?"

He nodded.

"Who's doing it?"

"Don't know. Wish to God I did. I'd . . ."

"Who tried to kill you? Start there."

"I have no idea. I can't remember much. I went to bed. Woke up strangling with a noose around my neck."

"That's it?"

"Look, either you'll look into it or you won't. And if you do you'll either find out someone's trying to kill me or I'm delusional as well as suicidal. You might even discover other murders disguised as suicides."

I thought about it.

"Ask the psych specialist about me. She'll tell you. I'm not like the other guys in here."

"Oh yeah?" I said, waiting for yet another insistence of innocence.

"I'm actually guilty. I had a severe drug and alcohol addiction. But I've been clean for over four years. I work my program hard. I get out soon. I've got a great job lined up. Family and friends waiting on me. I have absolutely no reason to kill myself."

"But you think someone does?" I asked.

"Must."

His young, unwrinkled face filled with worry lines as he frowned deeply.

"Any idea who?"

"None.

"Or why?"

"No, sir."

"Having problems with anyone?"

"Nothing major," he said. "Just the normal bullshit."

I nodded.

"Why don't you believe me?" he said. "Why're you so hesitant to help me? I thought you were different. I thought you—wait. There was a . . . in my . . . What if I can *prove* someone was trying to kill me?"

"Can you?"

"I just might," he said. "I think the killer may've left a calling card."

Chapter Nine

"It's gotta still be in my property," he said. "Go get it and I'll show you."

"Go get what?"

"My property."

Everything an inmate owned or was issued, such as uniforms and boots, was known as his property—and it was how everyone inside, both staff and inmates, referred to it. We even had a property room and a property sergeant.

"What is it?" I asked.

"Whoever tried to kill me slipped somethin' in my pocket," he said. "I'm sure it's still with my property now. Officers probably just thought it was mine."

"Thought what was?"

"I felt it in my pocket but I can't be sure what it was."

I walked over to Confinement and searched through Lance's property.

It took a while—not because he had so much. He didn't. But I was thorough, carefully going over every inch of everything he owned.

I wouldn't call my search a complete waste of time, because now I knew, but it yielded nothing helpful. There was nothing unusual or suspicious in the modest possessions the state of Florida allowed Lance to call his.

I walked back over to Medical angry and frustrated—and only partly at Phillips. I should've known better.

I was past the infirmary and nearly back to the SOS cell when I realized Lance had only one uniform. It didn't stand out because nearly all searches of inmate property involve only one uniform—the inmate was usually wearing the other. But all Lance had on at the moment was a canvas shroud—the only thing permitted in the SOS cell. So where was his other uniform? It was a good question. Worth asking.

"Where's Phillips's uniform?" I asked the small woman at the nurses' station. "The one he was wearing when he came in."

She shrugged without saying anything, which made her seem even younger.

She was a little less than five feet, so petite she probably did most of her shopping in the children's department, and I was sure her nurse uniform had to be special ordered—that or she sewed it herself.

"You have no idea?"

"Wait," she said, holding up her tiny hand. "Give me a minute."

"Take two," I said. "It's important."

"We bagged it up, but I don't think it's been sent anywhere yet. Let's see . . . Check the back counter of the infirmary."

I did.

As I walked back to the nurses' station, my

impatience ballooning, I tried to breathe up some zen.

"It wasn't there?" she asked.

"Amazingly, no. Any other ideas?"

"Wonder if this is it?"

Without standing up, without much movement at all, she reached over and grabbed a clear plastic bag with an inmate uniform in it.

I took the bag and began to empty its contents.

The tag sewn onto the shirt had Lance's full name and DC number on it. I looked through it, returned it, and withdrew his pants. A single playing card fell out and fluttered to the floor.

Returning the inmate blues to the bag, I handed it to the helpful nurse, and bent to retrieve the card.

It was from the Florida cold cases deck, a king of hearts—sponsoring agency seals on the back and information about Miguel Morales on the face.

"What do you know about Miguel Morales?" I asked.

I had just returned to the SOS cell from examining Lance's property and was sitting in the rickety old folding chair again.

He looked genuinely perplexed, his pale forehead making waves like a child's depiction of water. "Who? Did you find—"

"Morales," I said. "Miguel Morales."

"Never heard the name before. Who is he?"

"You don't know?"

He shook his head. "He who tried to kill me?"

"A missing person. Hispanic male. Last seen in Sarasota three years ago."

"What's that got to do with—"

"I'll be in touch," I said.

"What was in my pocket?"

I stood.

"You gonna look into this for me? I get out soon. I've worked real hard to be ready. I just want my second chance. I've almost made it. Don't let them kill me. Not when I'm so close. Please."

Chapter Ten

Suicide is an epidemic in prison.

And though it has been on a sharp decrease since the 1980s, it still accounts for more deaths in prison than murder, accidents, and drug and alcohol overdose combined.

In state and federal facilities, suicide accounts for about 6 percent of all deaths. In county jails it's much higher.

Because inmates don't have easy access to drugs or weapons, they often employ methods that are as creative as they are torturous. The three most common types are strangulation, poisoning, and self-inflicted wounds. Strangulation is the easiest, poisoning the most difficult, self-inflicted wounds the most brutal. With asphyxiation you drift off to sleep. With poisoning, toxic cleaning chemicals damage your kidneys beyond repair. But with self-inflicted wounds, you cut and rip and tear and gash your own skin with makeshift blades and sharp objects and wait to bleed out.

But maybe Lance Phillips didn't try to kill himself. Maybe there had been fewer suicides at PCI than we thought.

I looked at the cold-case king of hearts again.

One card didn't make for a good hand—no hand at all, in fact—but I was willing to bet on homicide over suicide, and I was counting on the property sergeant to reward my wager.

"Ever see one of these—" I began.

"Of course."

I was holding up the cold-case king of hearts.

"In the property of an inmate who supposedly committed suicide?"

"Oh."

The heavy makeup on Sergeant Carrie Helms's fifty-eight-year-old face emphasized rather than de-emphasized the laugh lines and wrinkles, but she had a youthful bearing, and her bright blue eyes still sparkled mischievously beneath her short gray hair.

She took the card and examined it.

Cold-case playing cards are created and distributed by several statewide law enforcement agencies, including the DOC, FDLE, sheriffs' and police chiefs' associations, and crime stoppers. Each deck features information about fifty-two unsolved homicides or missing person cases, with the crime stoppers toll-free tip line and the cold-case team web address. The decks are doled out to inmates in hopes they'll come forward with information that'll help solve the very, very cold cases.

Thinking about the cold-case cards triggered something inside me, and I thought I recalled seeing a deck mixed in among the other playing cards on the poker table in the farmhouse at Potter Farm this morning.

"Supposedly?" she repeated.

"Seen any of these?"

"I'm sure I have," she said. "These decks are all over the place."

"Not a deck," I said. "A single card."

Her eyebrows shot up, smoothing out the skin of her wrinkled forehead. "Hmm," she said, eyeing me with a conspiratorial expression. "I'd have to check. What's this about?"

"It was with Lance Phillips's property," I said. "Not the deck. Just the single card. He says whoever tried to kill him and make it look like suicide slipped it in his pocket."

She looked at the card again, reading the information about Miguel Morales who went missing in Sarasota three years ago.

"I'll only have the property of recent suicides," she said. "Older ones will already be gone."

"Do you mind checking?"

"It'll take a while. Probably tomorrow morning at the earliest. You think Phillips had something to do with Morales disappearing?"

I shrugged. "The killer might. Or maybe the card itself and not the cold-case info means something to the killer. Or maybe there's no killer."

"Know anything about the Morales case?"

I shook my head. "Will the next time you see me."

She smiled. "Never doubted that, John Jordan. Never doubted that."

Chapter Eleven

I stopped by the chapel on my way up to the warden's office and called Dad.

Chaplain Singer, the staff chaplain forced upon me by the new warden and the one he was working hard to give my job to, was out this week and I had the chapel to myself.

"Driver for Kent Clark says he's no hero," Dad said.

"Oh yeah?"

"Didn't try to stop the robbery of the body in the back of his hearse. Didn't even get much of a description or bother to write down the plate."

"What happened?"

"Says he was on a long, empty stretch of Highway 22 between Pottersville and Panama City when a nice black car pulls up beside him and a guy in a mask with a gun motions for him to pull over."

"What kind of mask? What kind of gun?"

"Halloween. Monster mask of some kind. Shotgun as best I can gather from his description. Says the guy told him he wouldn't hurt him. That he just wanted the girl. Took his keys and his phone. Tied his hands to the wheel. Took the body. Tried to stuff it in the trunk but it was too stiff. So laid it in the backseat. Tossed the driver's keys and phone into the woods and took off."

"He seem credible?" I asked.

"I find his incredibility credible. If he were faking stupidity or ineptitude, I think he'd bring it down several notches."

"What's his story?"

"Grandson of Kent or Clark. I forget which. Student at Gulf Coast. Musician. Just your general all around genius."

"What're y'all doing now?" I asked.

"Tryin' to figure out how to put out a BOLO for a *nice* black car."

I laughed.

"I have no idea what the hell is goin' on," he said, "but the body being stolen this way makes me think it's someone tryin' to embarrass me before the election."

"Could be," I said. "Whatever it is, we'll figure it out."

"What're you dealing with there?" he asked.

I told him.

When I finished, we were quiet a moment.

"Oh," I said, remembering something I wanted to ask him. "Is Jake with you?"

"No. Why?"

"When you see him would you ask him if one of the decks they were using in the poker game last night was a cold-case deck? And who brought it?"

"Sure. Why?"

I told him.

"I know you got a lot on you, son, but if you could help me with this thing . . . I'd be grateful."

"Of course," I said. "Absolutely. You got it. I was gonna see Mom during my lunch break, but if you need me to do something—"

"No, see her. If something comes up, I'll call you. Otherwise just check with me after work."

"I told you to be in my office first thing," Matson said. "This is the very thing I'm talkin' about. It's always somethin' with you. When I give an order I expect it to be followed to the letter. No exceptions."

We were in his office with the door closed.

Of course, that didn't prevent anyone outside his office or in the admin building from hearing what he was saying.

The office, like the man, was stark and severe, minimalist and utilitarian. Everything was institutional and state-issued except for a few framed photographs of inmates working on the farm at Angola, Florida and Louisiana DOC citations, some trite religious and motivational posters, and a little LSU memorabilia.

"I run my prisons a certain way," he said. "It's why I'm good at what I do. It's why I've been brought here. I'm going to whip PCI into shape and then it will be the model for the rest of the state. It takes a certain type of person to work at a Bat Matson institution. Not everyone's cut out for it. In fact, most people aren't. It's nothing personal. I just don't feel as though you are."

I started to say something but he stopped me.

"Just think about that last eighteen hours," he said. "I see you having an altercation with a respected attorney. Find you here in the middle of the night pretending to be a deputy sheriff. And when I tell you to be in my office first thing this morning, you show up over an hour late. Showing up late to work on a day like today of all days—"

"A day like today?"

"When I gave you an order to be in my office first thing."

"Oh, that kind of day," I said. "Actually, I wasn't late. I was early. I was called in to deal with an attempted suicide. I came to your office following that."

"Oh, well . . . okay then. But you should've gotten word to me."

"Sorry," I said. "I figured you knew."

I stopped short of saying I thought he knew everything that went on in his institution.

He started to lean back, but stopped and took a sip of coffee from a Styrofoam cup on the edge of his desk. The sip was loud, accompanied by various swallowing sounds—the kind made by the unselfconscious and uncouth. In big and small ways, Matson was the sort of man who gave no consideration to anyone else in the room. In any room anywhere.

When he did lean back in his chair, he straightened his tie.

I wasn't sure if the cheap black tie was the only one he owned or if all the ones he owned were identical to it, but he wore it or one like it every day. Black poly/cotton, flat-front work pants. Black Polyurethane lace-up shoes. White cotton shirt with button-down collar. Black too-wide tie. Never a coat. Never any variation. A self-styled uniform as severe as the middle-aged man wearing it.

"Now, on to these other matters," he said. "What do you know about the young woman killed last night?"

"Absolutely nothing."

"But—"

"I saw her a few minutes before I left Potter Farm," I said. "She seemed like she might need help. I gave her my card. I never even got her name. Did you see her?"

"*Me?*"

"At the farm I mean. When you were in the house or out in the pasture before you left?"

"Oh. May have. I'm not sure. So you don't know anything about her?"

I shook my head, wondering why he was so keen to know. It may have just been because she was found at the prison, but it seemed like more.

"And you got called because her card—I mean *your* card was in her . . . on her person?"

He seemed flustered, something I'd never seen before.

I nodded.

"Not because you're going to be investigating her death."

"I was called because of the card," I said.

"If you do your job the right way, there won't be any time left for anything else. And like I've said all along . . . if you want to be a detective then be that. You might be good at it—better than chaplain. Just stop trying to be both."

I didn't say anything.

"But the most troubling issue I needed to talk to you about is what Chris Taunton said at the gathering last night. I've asked around. I didn't just take his word for it. He was drinking . . . and I wanted to be sure. I'm now satisfied that I know the answer—and it appears to me that it goes far deeper than what he even accused you of. But I'll ask you directly. Are you living in sin with another man's wife?"

Phrasing it the way he had, the way so many do, made Anna sound like Chris's property, like he owned her, like the real question wasn't what we were doing but did we have his and society's permission to do it, did I have property rights to her.

One of the aspects of prison chaplaincy I liked most was the privacy it afforded me. Unlike when I pastored a church, as a chaplain I didn't live in a fishbowl, watched every second by parishioners who felt like they owned me and that I owed them. As a chaplain, my personal life was personal.

At least until now.

"I am not living in sin," I said.

What Anna and I had was sacred. There was nothing sinful about it. Matson was not the kind of man who could understand that.

Anna's relationship with Chris was over. We planned to marry as soon as her divorce was final, but we were not going to wait until then to be together. We had waited for far, far too long already.

"I'm sorry, sir, but I simply do not believe you."

Something inside me broke loose a bit and I just couldn't hold back any longer.

"Believe this," I said. "I've loved Anna Rodden my entire life and will love her for a million more lifetimes long after the sun has burned itself out and the universe has collapsed. Nothing will ever change that. Not Anna's duplicitous husband, not any laws of man or social conventions, not you or the Department of Corrections. My private, personal life is just that."

"No chaplain of mine is going to be shackin' up with another man's pregnant wife," he said. "Believe that. I've reported this to the chaplain supervisor of the state and the secretary of the department. I'm waiting to hear back from them on exactly how to proceed. Until then, do your job and nothing else. Understand?"

Chapter Twelve

"**S**ometimes I think about killing myself," Mom said.

I didn't say anything. Just listened.

"That surprise you?" she asked.

I shook my head.

Actually, my mom was already dying from suicide—the slow suicide of alcoholism, cirrhosis eating away at her body—her pickled brain and nervous system failing, shutting down. She had fought the good fight during her illness, she had regained her faith, her sobriety, and her family. But now she was weary, ready, it would seem, for complete surrender.

"You'd understand?" she asked, eyebrows raising slowly, unfocused eyes searching, entreating. "If I did, I mean."

I hesitated a moment, but then nodded, and said, "I would."

The downstairs room Mom had chosen to spend her final days in reminded me of a confinement cell. It had the same hopeless sense of isolation, the same smell of inactivity, of sleep, the same view of the world, of life passing by outside of here, happening everywhere but here.

"You'd be okay with it?"

I didn't want my mama to die. I didn't want to have

to face a world she wasn't in, though such a world wouldn't seem to be all that different from the one I inhabited now. She wasn't a big part of my life—and hadn't been for a very long time.

My visits to her sickroom, my vigils over her deathbed, that was the extent of our interaction and relationship.

"I would *understand*."

It was not the same thing, and she nodded that she caught the distinction.

Before I left the institution earlier, I had made several phone calls and had found no connection between Lance Phillips and Miguel Morales. I had also followed up on a few inquiries relating to the murder victim from the farm. Both cases fascinated me, but I was pushing them back, keeping them at bay as best I could, doing my best not to let them intrude into this moment with Mom.

"You don't think I should, do you?" she asked.

Mom had been so pretty once. Now, spent, her body older than its years, only occasionally did her eyes sparkle, her face brighten, the young girl she had been peek out of the infirmed old woman she had become.

"I think it's not for me to say."

"You think I'd go to hell?"

"Absolutely not."

"Certain?"

I nodded.

"Certain enough not to stop me?"

"Notions of punishment and reward are juvenile. There is only love."

I thought about the old notions of suicide being a mortal sin—the kind only committed by those who had despaired of God's mercy. Of how those who had committed it were refused religious burial, their loved ones left behind refused comfort and reassurance.

Of course, that she could even ask me if I thought she'd go to hell reminded me the notions weren't just old ones. I couldn't even think in those terms, and that she could made me feel like a failure.

"How can he sit by and watch me suffer like this?" she asked.

"Who?"

"God."

"Is that what you feel like is happening?" I asked.

She nodded her weak and weary head. "Sometimes."

"I'm sorry," I said.

"I know you are, and I appreciate it, but I'd really like to know what you think."

"Honestly, I don't think that's what's happening. I know there are no easy answers, but . . . The best is freedom, but even it falls short. Whatever the reason, I do believe—not just believe, *I've experienced*—God suffers *with* us. *For* us. Doesn't just watch us."

The pain and conflict I felt incarnated into knots in my stomach. I realized how hollow my words sounded, how inadequate they were. She was hurting so badly she wanted to die, and I had nothing much to offer her.

"I haven't experienced that," she said.

I nodded.

"Maybe I still will."

"I really think you will."

Tears formed in her eyes and she blinked several times. With an unsteady hand, she reached up and pushed her dry, brittle, early gray hair away from her pale face.

"How much pain are you in?" I asked. "We can—"

She shook her head, wiped at her tears. "It's not that. I'm okay. Physically."

She looked out the window a moment, but didn't seem to see anything.

Turning back to me, she said, "Most people don't see their death coming, but I get to lie here and watch its approach like I'm tied to a railroad track."

I nodded.

"That's what I want to end."

"I . . ."

"What?"

"It's just . . . if that's your reason . . . I think you'd miss out on so much."

"What?" she said, anger accenting the edges of her frail voice. "Pain? Suffering? Depression? Despair?"

"In part, yeah. For what's in and beyond them."

"You might feel different if you were in my place," she said.

I nodded. "You're probably right. But the truth is *I am*. We all are."

Her lips twisted up into a frown and she seemed to think about it.

"It's not the same."

"No," I said, "it's not. But think about the experience of God suffering with you, for you, you said you had yet to experience. I don't want you to miss out on that. And cutting your life short just might."

She nodded ever so slightly, more with her narrowing eyes than her head.

I glanced at the small table on the other side of her bed and saw amid the dirty dishes, TV remote, used tissues, and tiny brown prescription bottles, a copy of *Final Exit: The Practicalities of Self-Deliverance and Assisted Suicide for the Dying* by Derek Humphry.

"How much thought have you given this?" I asked, nodding toward the book.

She shrugged. "Some."

"Will you really think about what we've talked about?" I said. "Can we talk about it some more soon? Can we do that? Will you wait? Not do anything until we've talked it through some more? It's your decision, and I won't . . . I won't try to stop you once you've made it, but I don't want you making it alone or being alone or with a stranger if you decide to do it."

Tears began to stream down her cheeks as she nodded. "Promise."

She smiled, her moist cheeks gleaming in the midday light coming in the window beside her bed.

We had such a complicated relationship. She had never done a lot of parenting. Self-centeredness, vanity, addiction weren't qualities that lent themselves to motherhood. As an adult, I had been more of a parent to her than she had been to me, but she was the only mother I would ever have and I didn't want her to die, didn't want to lose her one second before I had to. But far more than that, I didn't want her to miss out on the truly transformative experiences being offered to her. Not now. Not when she had so little time left.

Chapter Thirteen

I ran into Melanie Sagal at the Dollar Store on my way home from work.

Anna had asked me to stop by and pick up a few things and I was glad she did.

A dark-complected girl in her late teens with dark, straight, stringy hair, a trim but curvy body, and extremely straight, extremely white teeth, Melanie—one of the girls at Potter Farm last night—was striking from a few feet away. Up close, a certain hardness, twitchiness, and insecurity undermined her attractiveness.

"I just want you to know I ain't no hooker," she said. "I got two kids and not a lot of options, you know? But I ain't for sale. I'm raising both of 'em on my own without a lick of child support from either of their sorry ass daddies and I do what I have to to take care of 'em. What mom worth anything wouldn't, right? But God knows my heart and knows I ain't no hooker."

I nodded.

She was wearing very short cutoffs that showed off her long, smooth, shapely legs, sandals that showed off sexy but uncared for feet, and a tight white spaghetti strap tank top camisole with no bra beneath that showed off both the curve of her breasts and her dark nipples.

Though it was September she was dressed for full-on July. In her defense, there's not as much difference between July and September in Florida as other places.

"I know you're not," I said.

"Really?"

"Of course."

"You're not just sayin' that?"

"I'm not."

"Good."

From where we stood at the front edge of the building, I could see the steady flow of people entering and exiting. Small-town folk, like me, who didn't have a lot of shopping options. Poor people, like me, with little or no discretionary income. Here to buy the basics and not much besides.

The Panhandle was largely an impoverished place. Particularly the small towns like Pottersville. There were the working poor like me. People who didn't subsist in poverty but did live from paycheck to paycheck with debt and virtually no disposable income. Then there were the extreme poor who wouldn't be able to eat were it not for food stamps, would be unable to survive were it not for assistance, people who had no discretionary anything, only desperation.

The immorality of income inequality in our country was as devastating as it was dangerous. The vanishing middle class meant there were mostly extremes now— high-end department stores for the wealthy and Dollar Stores for the rest of us. Both were booming while most everything in between was struggling. There were no exclusive or expensive shops or boutiques in Pottersville, but that didn't mean we lacked variety. There were three different Dollar Stores.

Of all my friends, family, and neighbors, none were struggling to survive because of laziness or lack of effort. The seemingly random and capricious nature of their struggle was due to lack of opportunity—that, and the greed of those pulling the levers of the great machine, who decided to keep such an obscene amount for themselves.

"So tell me about last night," I said.

"Creepy ol' Ronald Potter hired me and Carla Jean to come out and help host his party. Well, the party after the main party. Girls aren't allowed at that."

"Never have understood that," I said.

"Me either. Anyway, I've done this before . . . and it was good money and there's not much to it. Just sort of hang out and entertain the troops, so to speak. But here's the thing, and this is what it all comes down to for me and why I even considered doing it—we don't have to do anything we don't want to."

I nodded. "Such as?"

"The way he puts it is he pays us to be there. That's all. What we do while we're there is up to us. Now, don't get me wrong, we want everyone to have a good time so we'll get tipped and be invited back to the next one."

"So what kind of stuff do you do?"

"Bring 'em drinks. Dance with 'em. Show 'em our tits. Fool around if we want to—but only if we want to. And remember these are mostly old geezers. Doesn't take much. Oh, they talk big, but most of 'em can't do much of nothin'. Plus which they're all drinkin' so much."

I thought carefully how to word my next question.

"What sorts of things do they ask for?" I said. "In the back rooms?"

"Anything their wives won't do," she said. "Or don't do a lot. I'm not sayin' we do them. You asked what they ask for."

I nodded.

Because of how quickly I had to get ready this morning, I was dressed more casually than usual, and I wasn't wearing a clerical collar, for which I was grateful.

"Felix's wife won't go down on him and he loves gettin' head," she said.

She seemed to be warming to our conversation— something I wanted to encourage.

"What guy doesn't?" I said.

"I know, right? Some guys are happy to get anything. I feel funny talkin' to you about this."

"Please don't," I said. "I'm a man. I get it. And I'm not a cop."

"Cops are the worst," she said. "They expect you to do what they say and they're not nice about it. And they're usually rough."

"Jake?" I asked.

"He's not bad. Really. That other one was. Andrew Sullivan. Guy's a prick. Put his hands around my mouth and neck and tried to make me swallow. I pretended like I did then spit it in his face. I woulda caught a bad beating for that but Jake stepped in and saved me."

"He been violent with you before?" I asked.

"When he drinks."

"He was drinkin' last night?"

She nodded. "Big time."

I knew he was on duty because he was at the prison crime scene. I guess I never got close enough to smell it on him.

Across Main Street, at the drive-thru liquor store, an elderly man on a rusting, once green riding lawn mower pulled up to the window, cut the motor, and placed his order.

"Your dad, Judge Cox, and Mr. Hugh Glenn are

always perfect gentlemen," she said. "Your dad has never asked for anything. Judge either, except for one time when he had too much to drink and he begged me for anal before he puked and past out. Mr. Hugh . . ."

"What?"

"I can't say it."

"Sure you can. You can say anything. It's all important and it helps me."

"I can't see how this will help . . . but he just likes to sniff me while he . . . you know . . . touches himself. They're all good men. I'm glad they're our leaders. I think your dad's a good sheriff, but I think Mr. Hugh would make a good one too."

I nodded.

Balancing the suitcase of beer on the hood of his mower with one hand while steering the small back wheel with his other, the elderly man drove away, turning right on Second Street and disappearing behind the empty building that had once been a NAPA Auto Parts store.

"Ralph Long talks a lot, flirts, but never does anything. I think he's gay."

"Pretty sure he is," I said.

She looked around us then leaned in and lowered her voice. "The worst son of a bitch I've ever run across is Don Stockton."

I nodded.

"And it was just you and Carla Jean? I asked.

"Yep."

"Not the third woman, the blonde, that—"

"Have no idea who she was. Wasn't with us."

"Did you talk to her?"

She shook her head. "I think Carla Jean did. Hell, sounded like she let her in the house, but I never laid eyes on her. I'd talk to Ronald Potter. If he didn't hire her she may've just been crashin'. Whatever she was doing . . . it got her killed, didn't it?"

"It did."

"So scary."

I nodded.

"That could've been me."

"I'm glad it wasn't."

Her face softened and she smiled and turned her head. "Thank you. That's a sweet thing to say."

We were quiet a moment, then I said, "Did anyone leave for a while and come back? Did anything out of the ordinary happen? Anything suspicious or strange?"

"Seemed like everybody was comin' and goin' but I can't be too sure. I don't remember a lot. I think somebody drugged me."

Chapter Fourteen

"**Y**ou didn't tell me Chris was such an ass to you last night," Anna said.

"Told you I saw him."

She smiled. "Good point."

"Assumed you'd guess the rest," I said.

"I should have. How could I have been married to him?"

We were sitting on the small back porch of my—now *our* trailer—watching the river swirl its way toward the bay, the soft glow of the setting sun gently tinging everything gold, purple, and pumpkin.

Evening was palpably present in everything, the air, the quiet, the cool and calm.

"Tell me about your day," I said.

"Very, very ordinary. Missing you was the best and worst of it. Tell me about yours."

I did.

"So you're working on a murder where the victim is unknown and the body is stolen, an attempted suicide that might actually be attempted murder, a mother contemplating cutting short the little time she has left, and a warden who's gonna fire you for being with me?"

"You left out the only thing that matters."

"What's that?" she said.

"I get to come home to you."

"You do, you dear, sweet man, but are you sure you want me? I—"

"Never more certain of anything in my life."

"Even with a baby on board, a psycho ex in tow, and the sin factor that could cost you your job?"

"I've waited my whole life for you."

"But—"

"And it was worth the wait."

"Just so we're clear there, Mr. Jordan, you know I love you the same way, right? Just because I didn't get to declare it to the warden or choose you over my job . . . I love you with every single cell of me."

I breathed that in, then kissed her.

We kissed for a while. The desultory noises of the river slowly floating by were the only ones I could hear beside the sweet, heavy sound of blood passion in my ears.

And the wide world with all its constant cares and troubles waned away.

"He does know it's me, doesn't he?" she said eventually.

"Who? Knows what's you?"

"The warden. He knows it's me, right? Why isn't my job in jeopardy?"

I smiled. "Double standard, isn't it? I'm expected to have his religious and moral sensibilities whereas you are not."

"I worked so hard to save my marriage," she said, her gaze drifting, her voice growing wistful.

"We both did," I said.

Her attention returned to me, her eyes finding mine. "We really did."

We did, didn't we? It was easy to say—and it was what we both want to believe, but . . . I had no doubt she had done all she could, but had I? I would always wonder. It reminded me again I needed to call Susan.

"Let's get back to the warden's expectations . . ." she said. "I'm . . ."

"A whore, basically."

She liked that, her face lighting up, her big brown eyes shimmering with delight.

"His word?" she said, taking me in her hand. "I wouldn't want to fail to live up to expectations."

We began fumbling with each other's clothes, unable to wait until they were all the way off for the devouring to begin.

"I'm *your* whore," she whispered hoarsely, her voice delicious with desire. "I've always been. Do whatever you want to me."

I did.

Later that night, after Anna went to bed, I walked out under the night sky and began to pray.

The heavens above me were brilliant with a billion stars, the earth below me, dark and damp, and I could feel the beloved moving through me in the cool breeze.

I was grateful and so very glad to be alive, and I began there.

Thank you.

Thank you for letting me be here. Thank you for letting me be a part of all this. Thank you for Anna, for love, for what we have in each other, for the life we share.

It came to my mind to pray for Chris, but I wasn't ready to do that just yet. So I saved it, planning on coming back to him when I was a little further in and the better angels of my nature had had a chance to have more influence.

I then lifted up for several inmates I was counseling, sending health and healing and forgiveness and peace in their direction.

Next, I prayed for guidance and wisdom, for insight and patience, for help as a man, a chaplain, and an investigator.

I really had no idea what the hell I was doing and I needed help with everything every single step of the way.

For the next several minutes I practiced some mindful meditation and was just about to pray for Chris when Jake walked up.

"Hey," he yelled as he lunged out of the darkness at me.

I jumped and he got a good laugh out of it.

"You out here listening to the colors of the wind or some shit like that?" he said.

I laughed.

"I came to make sure you weren't drinkin' again," he said. "We got serious shit goin' down and we need you sober."

"If anything could drive me to drink, it's you," I said, "but so far so good."

We were quiet a moment and his demeanor changed.

"I wish to God I hadn't stayed," he said. "I do. And I probably shouldn't've fucked Melanie, but she's not underage. I don't care what you say, and that's all I did. I didn't have anything to do with anything else. I never even saw the girl that got killed. Never took anything or did anything illegal."

"I talked to Melanie about you this afternoon," I said.

"What'd she say?"

"That you have a little dick but you're a decent enough guy."

"What'd she really say?"

I told him.

"I been thinkin'," he said. "Well, first . . . do you suspect me?"

"Of some sort of mental deficiency? Yes."

"Seriously," he said. "Do you?"

I shook my head.

"True story?" he asked.

"True story."

"So I was thinking . . ." he said. "The killer had to leave to kill her and dump the body. That narrows it down to whoever left, right? So it's got to be whoever left between the time Carla Jean let her in and when she was found at the prison. That was Don Stockton, Andrew Sullivan, Ronald Potter, and Felix Maxwell. I mean, everyone left the table throughout the night, but they're the only ones that left the house. Sullivan was gone the longest. Then Stockton. But I think they were all gone long enough to do it."

"That's good thinking," I said. "We need to go over everybody's exact movements. Can you—"

My phone vibrated and I answered it.

"Chaplain Jordan?" the deep voice with the thick Southern accent said.

"Yeah?"

"I was asked by the OIC to call you in to the institution. An inmate in A-dorm's dead. Looks like he committed suicide."

When I ended the call, Jake said, "What's up?"

"Emergency at the prison," I said. "I have to go in. Will you write down everybody's movements through the night as best you can remember?"

"Will do."

"Oh, and did I notice a cold-case deck on the poker table?"

"Dad asked me about that," he said. "Got me thinkin'. There was a deck shuffled in by the end of the night but it wasn't there when we started. I have no idea how it got in and who brought it. Is it important?"

Chapter Fifteen

A-dorm at Potter Correctional Institution is an open-bay, military barrack–style inmate housing unit that serves as the orientation and honor dorm. In the shape of airplane wings, A-1 houses new inmates during their initial week of orientation, and A-2 houses inmates with the best adjustment to prison, the ones who act honorably.

To be selected for the sixty-four coveted positions in the honor dorm, an inmate can have no disciplinary reports, or DRs, and must have achieved above satisfactory on his gain time evaluations in his work and housing areas.

Suicide did not seem likely for the honor dorm.

All the inmates from A-2 had been moved into other dorms, the yard was closed, and only a handful of officers and officials were near the crime scene. The still and quiet dorm with its rows and rows of empty bunks looked like an abandoned post-Cold War military base that had not survived down-sizing.

Buzzed into the dorm near the raised and enclosed officers' station, I walked in between the row of double bunks against the wall to my right and the single bunks in the center of the dorm to my left, toward the back corner, which was the least visible in the dorm, especially at night.

When I arrived, a few of the officers milling around

gestured toward me. Nearly all encouraged me to "have a look."

I did.

On the back side of the last bunk—the point in the dorm that was furthermost from the officers' station—an inmate was hanging on a small piece of rope, probably the kind used to crank the lawnmowers by the outside grounds crews. The small rope had been looped around the post at the top of the bed.

The body of the inmate fell forward against the rope, his pale face puffy, his dry, swollen tongue protruding. His head hung loosely, his arms dangling down toward the ground. The tops of his feet and bottoms of his shins lay against the cold tile floor.

He was wearing a pair of white boxers and a white T-shirt, both of which had his name and DC number stamped on them. Danny Jacobs. One of the most faithful members of the inmate chapel choir.

Beginning just beneath his thighs and culminating in plum-colored feet, his legs were a gradient of lighter to darker purple.

One of the officers standing nearby said, "They found him when they turned the lights on this morning."

I wondered if the dorm officers had made rounds after lights out last night.

"He leave a note?" I asked.

"No," he said. "Everything's just like we found it."

"Is someone assigned to the top bunk?"

"Yeah," he said. "Phillips."

"Lance Phillips?"

"Uh huh."

"Jacobs has been sleeping in the top bunk since Phillips went to Medical," another officer offered.

It was at that moment that I realized how close in size and build Danny Jacobs and Lance Phillips were.

If the officers knew that Phillips was in Medical for supposedly attempting the same thing, they didn't say anything about it.

"Anybody see anything?"

"Say they didn't," the first officer said. "But if they did, we'll know soon enough. God knows inmates can't keep a secret."

"Chaplain, what the hell're you doin' down here?" Mark Lawson, the interim institutional inspector asked as he walked up behind us. "This is a friggin' crime scene."

"I was called in by the OIC," I said.

"*I'm* the one that told them to call you in," he said. "Not to come pretend like you're still a cop, but to act like a chaplain. To call this boy's family and let them know what's happened."

Mark Lawson had been the inspector of Potter Correctional Institution for about two months. Here on special assignment, while Pete Fortner was on medical leave, he was an ex-offender who had received a full pardon from the governor, and the son of the woman who was dating the regional director.

He had the bulky build of an inmate and pea-green prison tattoos on his forearms, which according to the hype was supposed to make him more accepted and respected by the inmate population. So far I hadn't seen any evidence that it was anything but hype.

"Nothing's to say I can't do both," I said.

"Yes there is," he said, stepping up a little too close. "*Me.* Not to mention the warden."

He held his arms like someone who had worked out so much that his muscles were too tight to allow them to straighten.

"Listen," he continued, "I know you used to be a cop. Pretty good one from what I hear. I know you used to help the other inspector 'cause . . . well, let's face it, he needed help, but while *I'm* inspector, you'll be a chaplain. *Just* a chaplain. I don't need any help. I know what I'm doing. Understand?"

I didn't say anything.

I was angry and embarrassed. My ego had flared up, and I had to get it under control.

I took a deep breath.

"Understand?" he said, his eyes wide and challenging.

"Yes," I said. "I'm sorry. It's your crime scene. When they called I just assumed they wanted me to—"

"If we need any help, we'll call you."

"What should I tell the family?" I asked. "Homicide or suicide?"

His eyes narrowed and his forehead seemed to cave in toward them in ridges like layers of a cavern. "*What?*" he asked. "You serious? Of course it's a suicide. It's obvious."

As I was leaving the dorm, the FDLE crime scene team was entering.

"You're headin' the wrong way," Sally said.

She was a tall tech with big blond hair, big glasses, and big teeth, who had played basketball in college. We had worked together on a few of these before.

"New sheriff," I said. "I'm being kicked out."

"His loss. Anything I need to know?"

"Check his pockets, will you? Let me know if you find anything."

"Will do."

Chapter Sixteen

"**M**y son didn't kill himself," Cheryl Jacobs said.

This after several minutes of sobbing uncontrollably.

Was it normal reactionary denial or something else? Was she saying what most do in the face of such news or, shocked mother or no, was she right, her son not both victim and murderer?

I had started to call her last night shortly after being kicked out of A-dorm, but decided to wait until morning.

It was early. I was back in my office after only a few hours' sleep. But I didn't want to take the risk of her finding out from one of Danny's friends once the dorm phones had been turned back on.

"I know my son . . . He's been . . . doing good. Finally getting a handle on everything and how it works in there. He's been going to church, making a few friends. His letters have been so hopeful."

I made a small noise to let her know I was listening.

"I guess you just think I'm in denial, but I'm not. I know my son. I just spoke with him a few days ago."

She paused for a moment, but I could tell she wasn't finished.

Outside my window, inmates streamed by on their way to the property room in the early morning sun of what promised to be a bright, clear, warmish September day.

"You probably think I'm just trailer trash," she said.

"No, ma'am. I—"

"What kind of woman raises a criminal? Right? Well, let me tell you. I'm a school teacher. I have a master's degree. Come from a good family. Danny just got mixed up in drugs and could never get out."

"I understand," I said. "Happens to a lot of people. I'm not unfamiliar with addiction myself."

There was complete silence on the line for a moment, and I thought she might have hung up, but eventually I heard her take a deep breath and let it out slowly.

"I'm sorry," she said, beginning to sniffle again. "I'm just upset. I . . . I'm . . . He can't be dead. It must be some sort of horrible mistake. Please let it be."

"I wish I could."

There was something about Cheryl Jacobs's voice—a profound sadness that was there before I gave her the worst news a parent can ever be given. It was rich with loss and pain and raw-boned life—one that resonated with resignation and regret.

The intensity of her voice combined with the clear line created an intimacy between us, as if she were in the room, not a town or two away.

"I just can't believe he's . . . " she continued. "Are you sure?"

"Yes, ma'am."

"My God," she said slowly, sighing, and in her words I heard the echo of *My God, my God. Why have you forsaken me?*

Mr. Smith, my elderly African-American inmate clerk, had been at PCI since it opened and was one of the most well-regarded men on the compound—by officers and inmates alike. In my time as chaplain here, he had been one of the most honorable men I had met. It was fitting that he was assigned to the honor dorm. It was also helpful.

He shuffled into my office, head bowed, back bent, the round bald spot that crowned his large head showing.

"You lookin' into Danny Jacobs's death?" he asked as he eased into the seat across from my desk.

"Very unofficially. New inspector and warden don't welcome my involvement."

"No, suh. Don't imagine they do. They not gonna last long. They'a screw up somethin' important and get a promotion."

"You obviously know how the department works."

"Whole world," he said. "The whole world."

We both sat in silence for a moment, thinking about, I assumed, the way of the world—I was. I was also admiring a man like Mr. Smith who could see so clearly.

"You know he's sleepin' in Lance Phillips bed last night," he said.

I nodded.

"And Phillips try the same thing in Confinement just a few nights ago."

"Coincidence?"

"Be a hell of one."

"It would."

He leaned forward in the chair because of his bent back and winced in pain—something he did every time he had to move. Over his left shoulder on the wall was a picture Susan, my ex-wife, had bought me. It was a black-and-white photo of a giant cathedral whose pews were city buildings and aisles were busy streets. It reminded her of what I often said quoting John Wesley, that the world was my parish. It was one of the few pieces of evidence that she was ever in my life.

Call her. Stop procrastinating. Do it as soon as Smith leaves.

"They's pretty tight," he said.

"Danny and Lance?" I asked.

He nodded.

"They seem suicidal to you?"

He shook his head. "But they both try it before."

"They *have*?"

He nodded. "Neither the type to finish it though."

"Why you think?"

"Not serious. That somethin' you wants to do, you do it."

I thought about what he was saying.

"Like so many punks around here, they use it to check in to a private cell for a weekend," he continued. "Or spends time with one of the hot psych specialists."

Inmates have a limited number of ways to exert any control over their lives.

"Problem with they bunks," he said, "can't see shit in that back corner, 'specially at night. Calls it lover's lane and up-the-back-alley . . . It where some of the mens go to hook up after lights out."

"Can you tell me who sleeps near there?"

He nodded. "I can have them come up here and see you."

"Even better. Thanks."

The front door of the chapel opened and inmates noisily rushed inside.

When the inmates didn't find Mr. Smith at his desk, they came to my door and stared through the narrow pane of glass. Mr. Smith waved them toward the chapel library and told them he'd be with them in a minute.

"Last night in A-dorm," I said. "What went on?"

"Ten o'clock, lights went out," he said. "TV in the day room turned off. Weekends and holidays lights still go out at ten, but the TV stay on to about two."

"How dark is it after lights out?"

"Pretty damn dim," he said. "They gots a few lights with yellow bulbs in them they turn on, but it's dim— 'specially back in lover's lane. Officers can't see it from they station."

"How quiet is it in A-dorm after lights out?"

"Very. We got mainly old cons, been around a while, know how to act, don't be makin' a bunch of racket like the jitterbugs. He was killed, had to be quiet."

"Could've drugged him," I said. "Or put him in a choke hold to put him to sleep—it's easier than most people think. Or they could've acted as if they were helping him stage a fake suicide and told him they would call for security, and then when he passed out they let him die. Who was on duty?"

"Foster and Davis."

"They obviously didn't make rounds," I said. "Or they'd've seen him."

He shrugged. "Don't know what they do after I go to sleep. Usually they make rounds at ten and then a little before eleven. Then the new shift come on at eleven and they make rounds sometime after that. Few times I couldn't sleep, I didn't see any officer out on the floor between, say, eleven-fifteen and maybe four-thirty."

"You think Jacobs committed suicide?" I asked.

He shrugged again. "Don't seem like the type. I don't know. My gut tellin' me somethin' might be wrong."

I smiled. "Mine's telling me the same thing."

When Mr. Smith left, I reached for my receiver. With my hand on it, I paused for a moment, took a breath, said a prayer, then lifted it and punched in Susan's number.

"Hello."

"Susan?"

"Who?"

"Susan Jordan," I said. "Daniels. Susan Daniels."

"Must have the wrong number," she said.

I repeated the number.

"Right number. Wrong person."

"You mind if I ask how long you've had this number?" I said.

"Few months," she said. "Six maybe."

Makes sense. That was around the last time I had called her.

Chapter Seventeen

"**I** take it this isn't a social call," Hahn Ling said.

We had dated briefly a few months back, so there was a time when a visit to her office was social.

She was an extremely petite young Asian-American woman of about five feet, with olive skin, shoulder-length straight, silky black hair, and big black eyes. She was one of three psych specialists at the institution, and so pretty she made her parents an argument for interracial relationships even the most strident racist would have to consider.

She closed the *Diagnostic and Statistical Manual of Mental Disorders* and returned it to the corner of her desk.

Sitting across from her reminded me just how young she looked. I had no idea how old she really was. She would never tell me her age.

"You here about the suicide last night?" she asked.

I nodded.

"Well, don't ask me. I'm clueless about human behavior. Though . . . if you're gonna commit suicide in prison, that's the way to do it. They just threaten to commit suicide or act suicidal, we're gonna place them in an SOS cell for observation. It's why we have so few suicides at this prison—that and the great mental health care I provide them. But if a guy really wants to do it, all he has to is act normal and when no one's looking do the deed."

"So Jacobs hadn't threatened anything?"

"Not a thing," she said, shaking her head.

Unlike me, Hahn kept her entire library in her office at the prison. Mine was strung out over every room of my trailer. Her books were neatly stacked on nice bookshelves that stood against every wall of her office. She had works by Freud, Jung, Rogers, Fromm, Erickson, and Zimbardo, and titles like *Social Psychology, Psychology and You, Short-Term Psychotherapies for Depression, Crime and Delinquency,* and *Child Sexual Abuse.*

"He seeing you for anything?" I asked.

She shook her head again. "I think Dr. Baldwin was seeing him. I can ask her for you, but it'd probably be better if you saw her. She can tell you a whole lot more about this than I can. She's worked inside prisons for over ten years. She teaches the suicide prevention class for the staff."

I noticed that mixed in among her psychology textbooks and testing and diagnostic manuals, she had numerous modern pop psychology books as well: works by Peck, Bradshaw, and Moore, none of which surprised me. What did surprise me were all the self-help relationship books—new additions since my last visit. I smiled when I saw the spine for *Ten Men Who Mess Up a Woman's Life.*

Following my gaze, she said, "*What?*"

"Am I one of the ten?"

"Huh?"

I pointed to the book.

"Of course not. You're one in seven billion. Wish we could've given it a real go."

"You think we didn't?" I asked.

She laughed. "You kidding? Of course we didn't.

Can't when one's heart already belongs to another."

"Sorry about that."

"No you're not," she said. "And now you're with her and all is right with the world."

"Are you . . . Do you want to talk about it?"

We hadn't dated much and had never gotten serious in any way, but maybe I had missed something that she needed to process.

"Said everything I had to say," she said.

"Would you say it again?"

"Wish we'd've gotten a real go. That's it. No big deal. You wanna know about suicide or not?"

I smiled at her.

She smiled back.

"I'm very cynical regarding suicide in general, but especially in prison," she said. "It's all about manipulation. About getting what they want. Most of the threats we get are from inmates in confinement, and every one of 'em are trying to get a transfer. That's what it's become—a way to get a transfer. It's not even a cry for attention or help, just a way to beat the system. Some of them even scratch at their wrists a little, but it's so superficial it's laughable. And yet we have to treat everyone the same as if it were a genuine threat."

I nodded.

"They're placed in the isolation cell," she continued. "Either by us or by Medical if it's at night and we're not here, in which case we have to see them within one hour of arriving at the institution the next morning. They get a complete physical, and we give them a complete mental status evaluation."

"You mind walking me through the procedures?"

"We have two isolation cells. S-1 and S-2. S-1 is for those who've made an actual attempt. S-2 is for those who've just made verbal threats. In S-1 they are monitored every fifteen minutes, S-2, every thirty. In both cells, they're in there naked and without any of their property. They're given a canvas shroud sewn with nylon thread, a canvas blanket, and a plastic mat on the bare floor. Usually, within two days they realize we're not going to transfer them and they're begging us to put them back in confinement."

"Which you do?"

"Which we do gladly. Even if they wanted to kill themselves in that situation it would be very difficult. They don't have anything to kill themselves with and they're being monitored so closely."

Where there weren't bookcases in Hahn's office, there was Oriental art, reproductions of paintings mostly— lotus leaves, dragonflies, bamboo, garden walls, figures engaged in conversation, Chinese symbols in black and red. All in inexpensive Dollar Store frames.

"The ones who successfully commit suicide in prison never threaten it?"

"Those're the more likely but there're exceptions."

"What about Jacobs?" I asked. "You think he committed suicide?"

A look of bewilderment crossed her face. "Don't have any reason not to. Do you?"

I told her about Lance Phillips.

"You think someone's trying to kill Phillips?"

"Finding the card gave his story a lot of credibility. Having someone about his size, sleeping in his bunk, killed in the same manner gives it even more."

Leaving Hahn's, I let my mind drift back over why the body of the woman killed at Potter Farm and found at the prison was stolen.

We had immediately jumped to the conclusion that it was the killer attempting to hide evidence, but what if it wasn't?

Why else steal a body?

Maybe it was about concealing the victim's identity and had nothing to do with evidence.

Who was she? Why was she there? Why show up uninvited to such an event? Or, if she was invited, who invited her? Was it just for a rendezvous with the inviter or was the invitee there as part of some sort of sinister scheme? To derail a campaign? Embarrass a candidate? For revenge of some stripe or another? Maybe a setup. Could her role have been about blackmail? Maybe instead of discrediting, it was about controlling a candidate. Blackmail not to get a candidate to drop out of a race but to control him once he was in office.

But why steal the body?

If not because who she was or some evidence left behind could connect her to the killer . . . then what?

What about necrophilia? Why hadn't that occurred to me before?

What if she was stolen for something unrelated to her murder at all?

It was a stretch. A big one. But the fact that I hadn't even thought about it until now bothered me.

Was the driver involved?

What else wasn't I thinking of?

Chapter Eighteen

On my way to Medical I stopped by the property room to see if Sergeant Helms had found any other cards in the property of inmates whose deaths were deemed suicide.

"Any joy?" I asked.

"I've only found one so far," she said. "The others must be further back than I thought—or just misfiled."

"Anything in the one you found?"

She shook her head. "A whole deck. Not a single. You find a link between Phillips and Morales?"

I shook my head. "Doesn't look like there is one."

"Sorry," she said. "Maybe I'll have better news for you later."

"Mind if I look at the deck you found?"

"Sure," she said. "Give me a sec. I'll grab it."

I waited while she found it. It wasn't quick.

Eventually she placed the deck on the counter. "Here ya go."

It was a cold-case deck like the card I found in Lance's pants pocket, but an earlier edition. Same concept. Same agencies. Different cases.

As Helms moved about sifting through the stacks of inmate property, I took out the deck and began to sort it according to suit.

When I had all the cold-case cards in order, I could see that none were missing. But I could see something else besides.

None of the cards were missing, true, but there was an extra one.

"What is it?" Helms asked.

"Extra card."

"Really?" she asked in surprise. "I should've looked closer. You think the killer . . . what?"

"If he put it in the victim's pocket or cell—anywhere in his property, whoever gathered his things could've stuck it with the other cards."

"What is it?"

"King of hearts," I said. "But a different crime. Murder of a white female in Naples. Which probably means the card is what's significant, not Miguel Morales. Morales just happened to be the king of hearts in the other deck."

"Unless there's a connection between them," she said.

"This is a much older edition," I said. "The case on this one is ten years older than Morales. And what are the chances they'd be on the same card? But you're right, we need to look into it."

She nodded. "But it's probably the card, not who's on it. We've got an honest to God murderer here."

"Lots of them, actually," I said.

She laughed. "You're right. Forgot where I was for a minute."

Before she could say anything else, her phone rang.

As she turned to get it, I looked at the card again, and began to get that little buzz, that addictive sensation somewhere inside, I always do at moments like these, when possibility turns into probability.

Helms thrust the receiver at me. "For you."

I took it. "Chaplain Jordan."

"Guess what I found in Jacobs's pocket?" Sally said.

"King of hearts playing card."

"I wish you were on this one, John, I really do," she said. "Interim inspector's an arrogant asshole."

According to a recent article I had read, most men in America don't have close male friends. They have co-workers, or golf buddies, or hunting or fishing or ball game partners, but they don't have friends—and certainly not a best friend.

That was most men. I was different. I had Merrill.

Merrill Monroe was my best friend—and had been for over twenty years.

I ran into him as I was entering the medical building. I was on my way to question one of the inmates who slept near Danny Jacobs the night of his death.

"How's your mom?"

I shook my head and frowned.

He said, "Anything I can do . . ."

"I know," I said. "Thank you."

As usual, Merrill's correctional officer uniform was neat and pressed and stretched tautly over his enormous muscular bulk. His dark black face glistened under a small patina of sweat in the mid-morning sun and his eyes were wide and had that wild look that made most people uncomfortable, especially if they were white.

"How you holdin' up?" he asked.

"Okay," I said, nodding. "I'm okay."

All around us, inmates were entering the medical building for sick call and morning meds and exiting to go back to their dorms or to work. Most of them were noisy—laughing loudly or yelling to one of their boys, until they saw Merrill. Then without his even looking at them, they grew quiet and respectful and either nodded or spoke as they walked by. He didn't acknowledge any of them.

We stood there for a while longer, neither of us with much to say, enjoying one another's company, and I thought how much more pleasant the prison was, my life was, because he was here.

"I . . . I just—" I began, but broke off.

"What is it?"

I had the urge to tell him just how much I loved and appreciated him, but resisted because of the environment we found ourselves in and how uncomfortable it would make him feel.

I hoped it wouldn't one day be an addition to a long list of things left unsaid I'd deeply regret.

I walked down the gleaming tile floor of the medical corridor, past the SOS cells and the infirmary, to the medical conference and break room. It was empty. After buying a Cherry Coke from the vending machine, I walked down the other hallway leading to the back exit and found Walter Williams rinsing a mop out in the caustic storage closet.

"'Sup, Preach?" he said when he saw me.

"Got a few questions for you," I said. "About Danny Jacobs."

"Don't know nothin' about no Danny Jacobs or anything else, and if I did, I ain't fool enough to be tellin' you."

"You sleep in the bunk right next to Jacobs, don't you?"

"Not anymore. Motherfucker checked himself outta here."

"You see anything?"

"That's all I'm sayin'," he said. "So don't waste my time."

Time's all he had. Prison time. The slowest moving, most elongated, most excruciating time humans had yet to create.

He switched off the spigot, slung the clean mop back down in the bucket of dirty water, and walked past me into the hallway.

"Anything you say'll stay between us."

He jerked around toward me. "I told you. Ain't sayin' shit. And you can't make me. Why don't you just leave shit the fuck alone? You gonna get your ass shanked."

He turned around quickly and bumped into Merrill, who had just walked up.

Merrill slapped him across the face with his open hand. It was a hard slap, and Williams stumbled back, clutching his cheek as he did.

"What the fuck?" he said, bowing up, but then quickly backing down and lowering his voice as Merrill came into focus.

I knew he would be helpful now and it made me once again question my convictions. I didn't believe in violence. At least I didn't want to. I didn't want the world to be a place of violence and dominance and the use and abuse of power. I believed in the noble tradition of non-violence that included Jesus and Gandhi and Martin Luther King, but I lived and worked in a world where in certain circumstances the use of force seemed the only option, the only solution.

"Chaplain's got some questions for you," he said. "You don't mind answering a few questions, do you?"

"No, Serg. 'Course not. What you wanna know?"

Merrill looked at him and shook his head.

"About Jacobs, right," Williams said. "He didn't seem suicidal to me. I mean, hell, he was always a little out there, but not all sad and shit. Night was pretty normal. We all went to bed. He woke up dead. That's all I know. I'm a heavy sleeper—you can ask the doc. I'm on medication that makes me sleep hard."

"He say goodbye to anyone or give any of his stuff away?" I asked.

"Don't think so. Didn't give shit to me. Somebody say he give his stuff away? Who got it?"

"Who else was around his bunk that night?" I asked.

"Brent Allen," he said. "He sleeps above me. So he was up there across from Jacobs. Jacobs was in Phillips's bunk. Lance come in real late from Medical, Jacobs was asleep, so he just get in Jacobs's bunk. Emile Rollins was on the other side on the top. No one was on the bottom of that one."

"Did Jacobs hang out with anyone that night? Anyone come to his bunk to talk to him?"

He closed his eyes, his face scrunching into what I assume was supposed to be deep thought. Finally, he shook his head and reopened his eyes. "Pretty much stuck to himself—'cept for the psych lady and the nurse."

"Which ones?"

"Nurse Lee seen him a lot. 'Specially since he got out of confinement, but no one saw him more than the psych lady. Doctor. What's her name?"

"Hahn?"

He shook his head.

"Lopez?"

"No, sir," he said. "The old ugly one."

"Baldwin?" I asked.

"Yeah," he said. "She was with him all the time. He always going up to her office. She always coming down to the dorm."

"They both came down the night of his death?"

"Yeah."

"Anyone else go near him that night?"

"Yeah," he said. "The serg in the dorm. Foster. He did rounds that night."

"He doesn't usually?"

He shook his head. "CO usually do it while the sergeant sit in the officers' station. Seem like he stop by Danny's bunk a time or two."

"Anyone else?"

"May've been. I didn't pay much attention to his life. Living my own."

"And doin' a damn fine job of it too," Merrill said.

"Anyway," Williams said, "Baldwin who you wanna talk to. She the one that always with him. She act like his damn mother or girlfriend or some shit like that."

Chapter Nineteen

"It's the policy of the Florida Department of Corrections to do all we can to prevent suicides," Bailey Baldwin said, beginning her suicide prevention class in the training building. "That means we all have to pay close attention to threats, gestures, and actual attempts. We have to take them seriously, even if we don't think they are. If you ever have any doubts, act on them. Refer them to us."

Bailey Baldwin, PhD, was the senior psychologist and the head of psychological services at PCI. She was DeLisa Lopez and Hahn Ling's supervisor, so I probably knew more about her than most. I knew, for instance, that she was moody and slightly paranoid and practiced CYA like a religion. I also knew she constantly had tumultuous, troubled relationships, and had probably been involved with every one of the *Ten Men Who Mess Up a Woman's Life* from Hahn's book. Many of them more than once.

"How can you know if an inmate is thinking of taking his own life?" she asked rhetorically. "Some of the most common indicators are: saying goodbye, giving away his things, writing letters to friends and loved ones. In essence, wrapping up his affairs. If you see any of these key indicators, call me."

She sounded to me as if she liked to hear herself

talk, and she did it with certain flair, but her hands shook slightly, and she didn't seem to know where to put them, and her searching eyes betrayed the fragility of the persona she was projecting.

She was standing behind a podium in the large, dull, utilitarian room, her voice echoing off the tile floor and white windowed walls. In front of her, correctional officers and a few assorted support staff personnel sat at rows of narrow tables—very few of them seeming to be paying attention to anything she was saying.

"Now let's talk about depression, the leading cause of actual suicide," she said, removing the red jacket that matched her skirt and unsteadily draping it over a nearby chair.

"Depression equals loss," she said. "Loss of interest, loss of energy, loss of concentration, loss of appetite—physical or sexual." A streak of crimson crawled up her neck when she said *sexual*, and the correctional officers, who had been nodding off, came to life, smiling and snickering.

It was obvious that, among other things, Bailey Baldwin was insecure and suffered from feelings of inferiority, something working in such close proximity to the sultry Lisa Lopez and the alluring Hahn Ling had to heighten.

"Sometimes," she continued, "a suicidal inmate will be agitated or restless, sometimes he'll be sluggish, and almost always he'll be pessimistic and hopeless.

"What I've just described is a dangerous time in the life of an inmate, but the *most* dangerous time is when he seems to feel better. It's when he gets a little better that he has the energy to kill himself."

She paused and looked around the room nervously.

"Any questions so far?" she asked when she seemed to lose her place in her notes.

The officers who comprised the majority of the class, sitting with their arms folded in front of them, many with their heads down, others whispering or laughing, didn't even acknowledge she had said anything.

"Okay," she said, still looking down at her notes. "Like I said, most threats or even attempts of suicide in prison are attempts at manipulating the system, usually in hopes of getting a transfer. However, others are cries for help, and all are dangerous. I can't tell you how many people kill themselves each year who don't actually mean to succeed at suicide. Self-injury and injury to staff is a serious matter, and if you observe any inmate displaying any of the characteristics I've mentioned, please, for God's sake, refer them to me."

When she dismissed the class, everyone scattered more quickly than at quitting time, and I walked up to where she was gathering her things.

"Hey, Chaplain," she said. "How're you?"

"Good, thanks," I said. "I enjoyed your presentation. Very informative. But I was surprised you didn't mention the suicide we had here last night."

She nodded as if she could see why I would wonder that. "I felt that it was too soon. And the truth is, we don't know enough about it yet. Perhaps with some time and distance . . . healing and objectivity will allow me to use it as an example, but that's a good question."

I wondered if she was going to pat me on the head.

"Was Jacobs undergoing psychological care?"

"Some," she said. "He tested well and didn't seem to be much of a threat to himself or anyone else. Sometimes that's the best we can do. It's a mystery. Death always is. Anyway, there will be a psychological autopsy to determine

what happened and why . . . see if there was anything else
we could've done. I doubt they'll find anything. I saw him
as often as I could—more often than his case required."

A psychological autopsy is a procedure for
investigating an inmate's death by reconstructing as much
as possible what the person thought, felt, and did prior to
taking his life. The reconstruction is based on information
gathered from classification, medical, and psych documents,
the institutional inspector's report, the ME's report, and
interviews with staff and inmates who had contact with
him leading up to his death.

"Did you see him last night before he died?" I asked.
She shook her head. "I don't believe I did."

"You sure?" I asked, trying not to sound accusatory.
"You were down in his dorm, weren't you?"

She looked up, seeming to concentrate all her mental
energies on remembering. "That's right. I *was* called in for
an emergency. And I did go to A-dorm, but I didn't see
Danny."

"You didn't?"

"I mean, I may have seen him, but I didn't speak to
him. I didn't see him as in having an appointment with him
or anything. Now that you mention it, I *did* see him talking
with Jamie Lee. Seemed fine at the time."

"What do you think happened?" I asked.

Tears filled her eyes. "We let him down. Just like
his family and society, we failed him. His blood's on our
hands."

Her maudlin sentiments came across as inauthentic,
even spurious. Was she merely saying what she thought she
should or trying to cover up something far more sinister
than insincerity?

After leaving training, I searched the institution
unsuccessfully for Donnie Foster, the sergeant on duty in

A-dorm the night Jacobs was killed.

When I called his home, his wife said he couldn't come to the phone. I left my number, though I knew he wouldn't call.

"He ain't done nothin'," his wife said.

"I just need to ask him some questions."

"What you *need* to do is leave him alone."

Chapter Twenty

After work I stopped by the courthouse.

Because there was a county commissioners meeting later in the evening, I might just be able to talk to several of the men from the farmhouse the night of the party, including Don Stockton, Ralph Long, Andrew Sullivan, Richard Cox, and Dad.

Built in the 70s, the Potter County Courthouse was bright and boxy, with light wood-paneled walls and white tile floors with black and brown and gold specks in them. A 70s-style staircase behind which was a fountain that no longer worked rose out of the lobby, leading to the second-floor courtroom.

The square box of a building had four equal hallways with offices off each side, and the sheriff's department and jail were located directly behind it in another, smaller square box.

I stopped by the property appraiser's office first.

I probably suspected Ralph Long as little as anyone. Not only was he harmless and effeminate with no interest in girls, but I doubted he had enough testosterone in his body required to beat someone to death.

"I was shocked to hear about that girl gettin' killed," he said. "Just couldn't believe it. And then somebody said her body was stolen out of the hearse. That's crazy."

"Did you see her?" I asked.

"When?"

I was a little surprised by his question.

"I meant that night, but anytime."

"You know, I think I did but I can't remember where. You know how your mind plays tricks on you. Memory's a funny thing. I thought I saw a glimpse of her in the house when I went to pee but I also think I remember seeing her outside as I was leaving. May not have been her. May not have been anyone. There wasn't much moon. Thought I saw her across the field a ways. Seemed to be stumbling. Thought she was drunk. What if she was injured?"

"Which direction was she headed in?"

"Toward the woods I think."

"Any idea what time it was?"

"Sorry man, I don't. Don't even know if I really saw it. She couldn't've been in the house and outside at the same time."

"It wasn't different times?"

"Well, not really. I went and peed and then left. Don't think she could've gotten across the field by then. Let alone gotten beaten up."

"Unless," I said, "it happened while she was in the house."

I made my way up the stairs and into the judge's chambers next.

Judge Cox was preparing to leave for the day but agreed to stay and talk to me—though not before asking me to close the door.

"I have to be so careful," he said. "And not just because of my position but my convictions. I do my very best to be an example of integrity and honesty, to truly live above reproach. Sometimes I'm too careful. This was one of those times. I could've driven. I wasn't drunk, wasn't even over the limit, but I rarely drink and I didn't want to take even the slightest chance that I was even close to the limit, so I called my kids. I wish I would've never even gone into the little farmhouse to wait. I wish my name wasn't even associated with any of this. Even so, I was long gone before any of it happened. Diane and Richie drove back out to get me. I felt bad. They hadn't been home long after takin' you, but . . ."

"Did you see her at any point?" I asked.

"Who?"

"The blonde girl who was killed."

He shook his head. "Don't think so. Did catch a glimpse of a girl in the back of the farmhouse but don't think she was blonde. I was sitting in the front room and it was hard to see. And it was only a short while before the kids came to collect me and my car. We were home before the late local news was off."

"Notice anything out of the ordinary? Anyone acting suspicious? Anything at all?"

He started shaking his head but stopped. "It's probably nothin'. And if none of this would've happened, I would've probably never thought of it again. As we were leaving, Diane's lights swept across the field and I saw Commissioner Stockton walking toward the woods. It's probably nothing and I'm not accusing him of anything. It's just . . . he had just been inside and to then to stumble out of the house and to be walking funny across the field toward nothin'."

"Not nothin'," I said. "The woods."

I found Don Stockton in the hallway heading toward the county commissioner's room.

"Got a minute?"

"Sure, pardner," he said as if I were his best buddy. "What can I do for you?"

"I'm tryin' to figure out what happened to the girl who was killed at Potter Farm and wondered if you had any ideas."

"Ideas? About what?"

"Who may've done it and why? Did you know her?"

"I never even saw her," he said. "Give me a name at least and I'll try to come up with somethin', but as it is . . . 'fraid I can't help you."

"Anybody acting out of the ordinary? Suspicious? Upset?"

"Not that I noticed . . . but wasn't really on the lookout for that sort of thing, you know? I's too busy takin' your brother's money."

"How much is he into you for?"

"We're square," he said. "He owes me nothin'."

"What were you doin' when you weren't doin' that?" I asked.

"That's about all I did," he said. "Winnin' that kind of money takes more'n a minute or two."

"But when you weren't at the table taking Jake's money, where'd you go and who'd you see?"

"Guess I got up to piss a time or two. Don't remember seein' much of nobody."

"Do you remember anybody leaving the house for a long period of time and coming back?"

"Didn't really notice, John, but even if I had, I don't think any of 'em are capable of killin' anybody—even a hooker—so I wouldn't point a finger of suspicion at 'em."

"Why do you think someone stole the body?" I asked.

"Reckon he wasn't finished with her," he said.

After leaving the courthouse, I walked over to the sheriff's department to discover that Andrew Sullivan was off duty, but Dad was in his office.

"Was hoping to talk to Sullivan," I said.

"Really? Why?"

"He was one of the ones at the after-party," I said. "And one of the few, according to Jake, who left long enough to have committed the murder and moved the body."

"I'll set up a time for us to talk to him."

"How long were you in there?"

"Where?"

"The farmhouse."

He shrugged. "Not too long. Shook a few hands. Said some thank yous. You suspect me?"

I shook my head. "Did you see the victim at any point?"

"Yeah," he said, "I was just waiting for the right time to mention it. No I didn't see her. I didn't see anything suspicious. I would've already said something if I had."

"Who was in there when you were?"

"Jake, Stockton, Andrew, Potter, and Felix were already playin' cards. If the girls were there they must've been in the back. I never saw any of them. Ralph Long was in there running his mouth a mile a minute but nobody was listening. The judge came in and sat for a while but not long. He left before I did. I don't remember anybody else but I wouldn't bet my life on it. Wasn't payin' too close attention. And I was exhausted."

"Nothing on the body yet?" I asked.

"Nothing. It's the strangest thing I've ever seen in all my time in law enforcement. It's just gone. Have you had any ideas where it might be?"

"Not any you haven't," I said. "Put out a description

to all agencies in the area. Check all the hospitals and morgues for Jane Does. Beyond that, I'm at a loss."

"Had any more thoughts on why the body was stolen?" he asked.

"See previous answer," I said. "None you haven't."

I then told him about some of the ideas that had occurred to me earlier in the afternoon as I was walking on the compound.

"The hell you say," he said. "That's several I didn't. Necrophilia never crossed my mind, you sick bastard."

Chapter Twenty-one

Later that night I drove.

As Anna and much of the world slept, I ran the roads.

I had too much on my mind, too many things to process, and I felt a restlessness I knew driving Anna's car would soothe.

Anna's car was a nearly new Mustang GT—another reason I was jonesin' to drive.

I was still driving a loaner, a tricked-out black 1985 Chevrolet Monte Carlo SS seized by the Potter County Sheriff's Department in a big drug bust. Dad had been letting me use it since I wrecked my truck while in pursuit of an escaped inmate.

The Monte Carlo, which had T-tops, pinstriping, a six-inch lift kit, twenty-six-inch chrome rims, illegally dark tinted windows, and a loud dual exhaust, was about as inconspicuous as Liberace at the First Baptist Church's annual children's piano recital, and I was sick of it.

Before I left, I created a new playlist for my ipod that fit my dark disposition, which included some Joan Osborne, Emmylou Harris, Jann Arden, and several covers of "Losing My Religion," "Ain't No Sunshine," "Paint it Black," and "California Dreaming."

The GT had a kickass sound system and I planned to take advantage of it.

As soon as I was on the dark rural highway leading out of Pottersville, I cranked the volume and opened her up, the haunting, mournful sounds of Emmylou Harris's "Wrecking Ball" a pitch-perfect match for my melancholic mood.

The leather seats seemed to mold to me, holding me in the cockpit-like interior of the iconic car. It'd been a while since I'd driven a powerful automobile, and I'd forgotten just how much fun it could be—especially when equipped with a stick.

The night was dark, only a shadowed rim of moon in a black, starless sky. A low-lying fog hovered just above the highway, the headlights of the GT piercing it, the beams followed hard by the racing pony behind them.

My mind roamed freely.

Anna, love, happiness, the attempt on Lance Phillips, the deaths of Danny Jacobs and the girl at Potter Farm, the cold-case cards, Susan, Chris, Matson, the body propped on the prison fence, Atlanta, always Atlanta, Mom contemplating taking her own life—all shuffling around randomly, then, suddenly, raining down on the green-top table like a deck that got away from the dealer.

I had lost many battles to the noonday demon of depression, but never the war. Never, not even at my lowest, wanted to kill myself. It hadn't ever even really crossed my mind, at least not in any kind of serious way.

Eventually I reached highway 98 and turned east, heading down the coast.

For a while I tried to figure out the significance of the cards left by the killer, but eventually gave it up and let my mind wander again.

Arbitrary bits bouncing around my brain.

Atlanta. Wayne Williams. LaMarcus. Martin. Jordan. Stone Mountain. The Stone Cold Killer.

PCI. Molly. Nicole. Tom Daniels. Laura Mathers. Justin Menge.

From a now obscure religion class—Confucius teaches there are three ways to learn wisdom: observation, which is noblest; imitation, which is easiest; and experience, which is bitterest.

Paul Tillich's God above God, what I would call God beyond God. The remembered pleasure of first reading Hemingway and Shakespeare and Graham Greene.

When lights from the city could only be seen in my rearview, I turned off the music and rolled down the windows to listen to the music of the night.

The wind whipped in and out and around the car.

Gulf to my right, slash pine forest to my left, empty road ahead. Waves rolling in and out. Rubber tires on damp asphalt.

Alone.

I found it interesting that at every empty convenience store I passed, the solitary clerks were outside—standing or sitting, smoking or not—all staring off into the distance of the lonely night. Was that which drove them out of the overly lit stores into the dark nights the same thing driving me down the fog-covered highway?

When I reached Port St. Joe, I rode by Cheryl Jacobs's house on Monument Avenue. Not sure why exactly. Was this where I was unconsciously headed all along?

Her house was a small, square red brick box of a dwelling on a large grass lot absent any landscaping.

To my surprise, no cars filled her driveway or lined her front yard, and through the huge bay window front, I could see she was alone, pacing around, a glass of wine in her hand.

I parked next to the curb in front of her house, pulled out my phone, and tapped in her number.

"It's John Jordan. Are you okay?"

"No."

"You really shouldn't be alone right now."

"How'd you know I'm— Where are you?"

"Out front."

"What're you doin' here?"

"I'm not sure."

"Come in."

Chapter Twenty-two

The little light above her front door came on.

I got out of the car and walked up to find her standing in the now open doorway. She was younger than I expected, and pretty, but she looked as if she had packed a lot of living in her short life.

Merrill always said, it's not the age, but the mileage. As was usually the case, he was right.

"I can't believe you're here," she said.

"Me either. I was out driving. Wound up here. When I saw you were alone, I called."

"I'm glad you did. Come in."

I followed her into the small, simply decorated house. It was quiet—too quiet, and perfectly still.

Standing on old but clean carpet, we were surrounded by pictures of Danny hanging from the thin, blond paneling—Danny's various yearbook pictures, Danny in his football uniform, Danny and date leaving for the prom, Danny and his mother, portraits and snapshots of a life lived largely together.

Through an opening above a bar top, I could see her kitchen was empty—no boxes of fried chicken and biscuits, no trays of sandwiches, no Tupperware containers of baked goods, no aluminum pie plates with half-eaten apple

and pecan and peach pies in them—nothing a grieving
house in the South should have.

"Why are you alone?"

"There are people," she said. "They would come."

I started to say something, then decided to wait.

Beyond a hint of hardness etched on her face, her
eyes shone kind and intelligent, and, of course, sad. So very
sad.

"I got pregnant at sixteen," she said. "Kid with
a kid. Paid a hell of a price around here for that. Little
slut. Single mom. But I got through it. Went to college.
Eventually both Danny and I were accepted. But when he
got in trouble, it started all over again, and I just couldn't . . .
Everyone acted like he was dead when he went to prison . . .
That's when he died for them. No need to tell them now.
I'm alone in this tonight because I've been alone in this
since he went to prison. Nobody's here because I didn't tell
anybody."

"I'm sorry."

The house smelled of loneliness—not bad, just
empty—as if one person weren't enough to stir the air
around or make enough odors for the environment to
notice.

She shrugged. "Doesn't matter. What if it did?"

I smiled and nodded, and thought how many times I
had said those same words.

"We're all alone anyway. I mean, really. Aren't we?"

"We are."

"Still, I'm glad you're here."

"Me too."

"I still can't believe—"

She wobbled as her knees began to buckle and I
stepped toward her.

"Hug me."

I did.

Standing in the middle of her dim, sparsely decorated living room, I wrapped her in my arms and held her tight.

At first, small tremors ran through her, then she began to shake, then came the sobs, the deep anguished cries, and through it all I just held her. At a certain point, her knees buckled and she collapsed, pulling me down with her, but I never let go.

On the floor, I pulled her even closer to me, felt her tears and snot on my face and shirt. All I could do was hold her, so I did.

There is no sound more desolate, more disquieting than that of a mother mourning the loss of her child. A voice is heard in Ramah, mourning and great weeping, Rachel weeping for her children and refusing to be comforted because her children are no more.

After a very long time, her sobs turned to gasps, then to sniffles.

Then, as if suddenly and inconsolably embarrassed, she shrugged me off, pushed herself up, tried to stand, fell again, this time on top of me.

"Sorry," she said. "For . . . everything. I'm a mess. I just . . ."

"You have nothing to be sorry about."

"Will you help me up?" she said.

"Of course," I said.

And then I did.

"Tell me he didn't kill himself," she said when we were standing again.

"I don't think he did."

She hugged me.

"Oh thank God for that. I know it sounds so silly. Doesn't change anything, does it, but it means so much to me that he wasn't so tortured, so desperate, so alone that he took his own life."

"It's not silly at all."

She wobbled again, and I helped her over to the couch and eased her down onto it.

Laying her head back, she closed her eyes and began to breathe like she were falling asleep.

"Have you eaten?" I asked.

Opening her eyes drowsily and squinting up at me, she shook her head.

In another moment, she was out hard, snoring and still half crying in her sleep. Scrounging around her small, sad house, I found a pillow and placed it under her head, and a blanket and draped it over her.

I then went into the kitchen to make her something to eat and drink.

As I rummaged around her kitchen, I saw a pack of cards in a catchall drawer. They were above a pad full of solitaire scores, which made me sad for Cheryl.

The kitchen was small, its appliances dated, its linoleum worn, the varnish of its thin, homemade cabinets fading.

I began to think about the significance of the king of hearts again.

Withdrawing the cards from the drawer, I spread them out on the countertop and looked through them. When I came to the king of hearts it hit me immediately.

I should've seen it earlier. It was so simple, so obvious. I wasn't sure why I hadn't.

Unlike the cold-case decks, which featured a missing person instead of the king, this deck had the actual king— the suicide king.

The king of hearts is also referred to as the suicide king because he's sometimes pictured holding a knife to the back of his neck or actually stabbed into his head. Originally, the king had an axe, but over the years, the head of the axe was dropped from the picture. What remains looks like a sword—looks like the king is either holding the sword behind or stabbing himself in the head.

With limited resources inside, the killer would have to use whatever he could find. The cold-case king of hearts had to stand in for the suicide king.

The message was simple. You think these are suicides, but they're not. They're murders. I'm smarter than you. I'm the suicide king.

"What're you doin'?"

I turned around to see Cheryl standing in the doorway, wearing a thick, light pink terrycloth robe.

"Getting you something to eat and drink."

"And playing solitaire?"

I laughed. "Trying to work something out. The king of hearts have any significance to Danny or to you?"

She shook her head and shrugged. "Not that I know of. Why?"

"No reason. Just a random, idle thought. Can you eat?"

"A little. Maybe."

"Have a seat."

"Thank you."

"Sure."

"No. For being here. For . . ."

She looked at me and our eyes locked.

I nodded. "My pleasure."

I thought she might start crying again, but she didn't.

I stayed with her for another hour or so, then drove home.

Crawling into the warm bed with Anna felt like something I had meant to be doing my entire life.

She roused and we began to kiss.

"Thank you," I said.

"For?"

"The use of that amazing machine," I said.

"Anytime."

"It was an incredible ride. Just what I needed. As I was riding back I got to thinking . . . it cost more than my home."

"Our home," she said.

"That's sweet. We'll find a better place to call our own soon."

"I like it here," she said.

"You're perfect," I said, and I meant it.

"Whose perfume are you wearing?" she asked.

"Cheryl Jacobs," I said.

"Who?"

I told her.

"I just got out of a marriage with a man who cheated on me," she said.

Oh shit. How stupid could I be? I didn't even think about that. I wasn't usually this thoughtless and unaware.

"Who dealt duplicitously with me in nearly every way," she added.

"I'm so sorry," I said. "I didn't even think about—"

"It's so nice to be with someone I can trust," she said. "Such a great fuckin' feelin'. I know you John, know your soul, know the force of your character. You didn't think about it because you're not a cheater. You were out there doing good—either as a minister or an investigator. It's what you do. It's all you do."

"Still," I said, "it was inconsiderate. Thoughtless. I'm sorry."

She reached up and touched my face.

"I will never cheat on you," I said. "Not ever. You can count on that."

"I do."

"And I'll try not to make another rookie mistake like that again."

"Come on," she said, and I could hear a smile in her voice, "neither of us are rookies."

"Why it's all the more inexcusable."

It felt like I had just fallen asleep, and maybe I had.

My phone began ringing. I fumbled to find it on the nightstand, Anna rolling over and groaning beside me.

"You ain't gonna believe this shit," Merrill said.

"That you're callin' me at this hour," I said.

"No, not that shit."

"Then what?"

"Oh," he said, as if just remembering something, "Sergeant Helms say tell you she found cards in the other inmates' property. Say they were regular kings."

"Thanks."

"But that ain't the shit you ain't gonna believe."

"Well, go ahead and get to that shit," I said.

"Know how everybody say Brent Allen was hanging out with Phillips and Jacobs, how he sleep close to them?"

"Yeah?" I said, trying to talk softly.

"Guess what the bitch's nickname is?"

I didn't say anything, just waited.

"Go on and do it. Guess."

"Too early."

"His ass is known as the Suicide King."

"What?"

"Told you it some shit."

I laughed.

"Say the little fucker know everything they is to know about suicide. Say he tried a few dozen times too. *I say, he ain't trying hard enough.*"

Chapter Twenty-three

The laundry department at Potter Correctional Institution washed, dried, ironed, and folded the uniforms, towels, and sheets for some thirty-four hundred inmates every day of the work week. It was twice as big as any dry cleaners or Laundromat I had ever seen on the street.

Outside, the laundry building looked like all the other structures of the institution—nondescript gray cinder block with pale blue trim.

Inside, it was a large open space filled with huge commercial washers and dryers with a network of metal pipes and wires snaking along the steel structure supporting the unfinished ceiling. The building was also filled with noise. The hum of motors, the rush of fan-blown wind, the stamp of the press, the whistle of the steam, and the continual metallic slaps and clanks obscured every other sound made by the officers and inmates working among them.

"I knew you'd get around to me eventually," Brent Allen yelled above the noise when Merrill and I walked up.

He stretched a shirt between the two steaming halves of the press and pulled the lever releasing the top onto the bottom one and the wrinkled cotton fabric between them.

"Oh yeah?"

He shook his head. "Shame about poor Danny."

Brent Allen was a short, thick guy with a certain softness about him. His closely cropped brown hair stood on end and his copper eyes were dim, rimmed by puffy dark half-circles beneath them.

"What made you think I'd come see you?" I asked.

He smiled. "Come on, Chaplain. Don't treat me like the rest of the tards 'round here. I deserve better than that. Everybody knows I'm the go-to guy for all things suicide."

"You the damn Suicide King," Merrill said.

"One of 'em."

"*One?*" I asked.

"Yeah."

"There are others?" I asked.

"How can you have more than one king?" Merrill asked.

"It's a club," he said. "Or used to be."

"A *club?*" Merrill said. "What? Y'all play chess and shit?"

"A suicide club," Allen said. "Long time ago. We haven't even talked about it in—"

"Start from the beginning," I said.

"A group of us formed a club. Called ourselves the Suicide Kings."

This is it, I thought, feeling the buzz begin again. We're getting somewhere now.

"Who?" I asked. "Was Danny Jacobs in it?"

"It was a long time ago. Some of the guys have transferred. A few're already out. I'm tellin' you . . . we don't even . . . it wasn't even serious back then. Not really. And that's been . . . I don't know . . . years."

"*Was* Danny in it?"

He nodded. "But I'm telling you—it didn't mean

anything back then. Means even less now. It has nothing to do with him or his . . . "

"Who else? Phillips?"

"Yeah. Lance. Emile Rollins . . . ah . . . I can't even remember who else."

"Tell me about the club."

"We all felt suicidal . . . I don't know. We were like, fuck it. If we ever decide to go through with it, we could count on the others to help us out. Look after our shit. We made wills. Left each other our earthly possessions—even took out life insurance, but the policies had a suicide clause, wouldn't pay if the insured committed suicide."

"How long ago was that?"

"I told you. A while."

"Be more specific."

"Why?"

"The suicide clause on most policies is two years. If it happens after two years, they usually pay."

His eyes widened as his eyebrows arched and his forehead wrinkled.

"How long's it been?"

"About two years—but I'm sure they've all lapsed by now. We haven't been paying them."

"You didn't think you should tell someone about all this after the attempt on Lance or Danny's death?"

"Danny killing himself or Lance trying has nothing to do with a defunct club from a few years ago."

"And if they didn't do it to themselves?"

He stopped suddenly, holding the blue inmate shirt dangerously close to the press, the steam enveloping his hand. Squinting in concentration, he looked off into the open space of the laundry building.

"You think someone killed Danny?"

He had stopped squinting now, and his eyes twitched

and blinked as he talked.

"Do *you*?" Merrill said.

"I hadn't," he said, closing his eyes completely for a moment. "But if someone was trying to kill Lance . . . then they killed Danny by mistake. What does Lance say?"

"That he didn't try to kill himself," I said.

To our left, a group of about seven inmates stood around tables folding towels, while behind us inmates were loading and unloading towels and uniforms into the giant washers and dryers, all under the careful supervision of the laundry sergeant.

"Oh, that's a beauty," he said, shaking his head. "Kill someone who's attempted suicide before and make it look like suicide again. That's fuckin' genius. Who would suspect? I mean, think about it, if they hadn't failed to off him the first time and left him to say that he didn't do it, then no one would even question it. Especially in here. Hell, I bet no one believes him as it is."

His response to what I was saying was one of interest but not concern. If he cared for Lance or Danny, his fellow Suicide Kings, he didn't show it, and the longer we talked, the more he twitched and blinked. He looked like someone with shell shock or a nervous disorder.

Across the building, I saw the colonel duck beneath the half-opened rolling bay door and enter the laundry. The sergeant cleared his throat and the inmates sitting on the gigantic blue sheet press stood up and acted like they were working. The inmates sitting behind the sewing machines couldn't pretend to be busy because there was nothing on their tables to be sewn.

"Can you think of any reason anyone would want to kill Lance?" I asked.

"Sure," he said with a half shrug. "Lots of reasons to kill people. People've killed over some pretty petty shit before—'specially in here."

"Anyone in particular come to mind?"

"Not at the moment."

"Any reason why anyone would want to kill Danny?"

Brent Allen's inmate uniform looked new. Unlike the other uniforms on the compound, it wasn't worn and faded from wear and washing. It was also military crisp without a single wrinkle, pucker, or gather.

"Not as many as with Lance," he said. "Danny was quieter. Stayed to himself mostly. Actually, he's the kind I'd suspect of a legitimate suicide."

"Really?"

"You know much about suicide?" he asked.

He started pressing the shirts and pants of the blue inmate uniforms again, laying each garment down between the two small ironing board–shaped halves of the press, pushing the button, and waiting for the hydraulic press to drop, press, and rise again.

"Not enough to be called a Suicide King."

He smiled. "Suicide's sorta my hobby. It was a fad for the other members of the club, but for me . . . I probably know more about it than anyone. Want a quick class on it?"

I nodded.

"Well, first of all it's all bullshit."

"What is?" I asked.

"Everything," he said. "Everything people think they know about it. Everything I'm about to tell you. First thing to know is we don't know shit about it. Oh, the professionals say they do but they don't. They don't know why more people kill themselves than kill others. They don't know why more women attempt it, but more men complete it. They don't know why so few leave notes. They sure as hell don't know what was going through the poor bastard's mind at the end. Hell, I've tried it over a dozen times and I couldn't tell you what was going through mine. And they can't tell you why people choose to do it the way they do."

As we continued to talk, Allen's twitch moved out of his eyes, down his face, and into his body. Now he was shrugging his shoulders, slinging his arms, and jerking his head about.

Over the tops of laundry carts, some piled high with folded stacks of clean clothes and others with mounds of unfolded dirty ones, I could see Donnie Foster, the sergeant on duty in A-dorm the night Jacobs was killed, enter the building, look at us, and then walk out quickly, bumping into the inmates waiting to push the laundry carts back to the dorms as he did.

"Suicide's not bullshit," he said. "Everything else is. Suicide's the only sane response to this painful, meaningless disaster we're clinging to. For fuck sake, can you imagine a worse world? All we do is suffer and watch those we care about suffer. We lose everything—*every single thing*—including ourselves. How can any thinking person look at this cluster fuck of a world and conclude anything but that it's the cruelest joke ever played on anyone. Ever."

"How'd you do it?" I asked.

"Huh?"

"How'd you try to do the sane thing?"

"Every way in the book," he said. "And yes, there are books about it. Lots of 'em. We can't have them in here, but I have 'em all at home."

He unbuttoned the perfectly pressed left sleeve of his shirt with an unsteady hand and rolled it up. Long, uneven mounds of scar tissue like small worms beneath his skin ran along the bottom side of his twitching wrists. "Razor," he said. He continued rolling his sleeve up to

reveal the track marks on his arms. "Overdose." He then
reached up and tugged on his collar. Around his neck were
rings of scars and bruises—old scars and new rope burns.
"Hanging." Carefully unbuttoning his neat, clean, crisp
shirt, he exposed a thin white scar on his side. "Knife."

"If you were trying to qualify yourself as an expert
on the subject," I said, "you've succeeded."

"I've also tried pills, poison, carbon monoxide,
plastic bag, cyanide, self-starvation, and gunshot," he said,
pushing his hair back to reveal an old gunshot scar over his
ear. "And it's all still a mystery to me. Like death or life or
God. It's a mystery. People think if they could just know
what the guy was thinking . . . But all they have to do is ask
us and we could tell them. We don't know. We can't tell you.
Those who've done it couldn't tell you if they were here."

I nodded, but didn't say anything.

"The number of suicides each year is probably five
times greater than what we think," he said. "Most anybody
is capable of it under the right circumstances. And the
decision to do it is usually a cumulative one. So when
someone takes his life, it's because of a buildup of several
factors, none of which by themselves would cause him
to do it. You've heard of the straw that broke the camel's
back, well, that's how it happens. You have all this shit and
it just keeps piling up on you and then maybe it levels out.
Maybe for a long time. But then this one tiny little thing
comes along, and maybe it's nothing. Maybe it doesn't
amount to a tiny piece of straw, but it's the final straw and
it's just too much to handle, so you go for it."

"And you don't see evidence of that in Lance's or
Danny's lives?"

He shook his head. "But all sorts of people commit
suicide. There's no profile. Think about the difference
between Hitler and Hemingway or Judas and Juliet and yet

they all did it."

"You know so much," Merrill said, "why you so unsuccessful at it?"

"What I do is about luck, not skill. Everything to do with chance. The universe is such a random place, I . . . my attempts contain the possibility for intervention. I let fate decide."

"*Sheeit*," Merrill said. "You really think fate wants your sorry ass around?"

Chapter Twenty-four

"The killer's calling card didn't make you think you should tell me about your little club?"

I'd found Lance Phillips in line at the barbershop and called him over away from the other inmates waiting for a bad buzz cut.

"Huh?" Lance said.

He looked around constantly, scanning the compound. He was obviously nervous, distracted, scared.

It was a brilliant, beautiful September day, and the compound was abuzz, inmates swarming about like bees at the height of tupelo season.

"I felt it in my pocket," he said. "Tried to look at it, but couldn't make it out. I was nearly unconscious."

"It was a playing card."

"Oh."

"From the cold-case deck. Had a missing person on it."

All around us, inmates were moving—in and out of dorms, in and out of canteen lines, in and out of the barbershop. A steady stream of them flowed toward the center gate and a steady stream flowed back. Cigarettes were being rolled, trash was being talked, deals were being made, and everywhere seen and unseen, intentional and not, threats, slights, disses were being both issued and noted.

"Miguel what's-his-name you mentioned?"

"Morales. Yeah. What's your connection with him?"

"None. I mean, that I know of. I've never—"

"Card was a king of hearts. That mean anything to you?"

He shook his head. "Should it? You know who tried to kill me?"

"Forget about the cold-case deck for a minute," I said. "In a regular deck the king of hearts is also known as—"

"Oh fuck me," he said, his eyes growing wide and even more fearful. "You think this has something to do with the Suicide Kings?"

"Whatta you think?"

"But why not put a suicide king in my pocket? Why the one with Miguel Morales?"

"Maybe that's all he had at the time," I said. "He put a regular suicide king in Danny's pocket."

He looked down and frowned, his eyes busy blinking back tears, but only for a moment, then he was back to scanning the passing inmates, looking over his shoulder.

"They tell you I found him?"

I shook my head. Not telling me much of anything.

"I got out of Medical very late. He was already in my bunk asleep. He got in it a lot. I've got a thicker roll, more comfortable—guys always trying to sleep in my rack, but Danny just always felt safer up there. I didn't mind. I left him in it—just got in his. Did that get him killed? That would be . . . I don't know, ironic. Man that's . . . I didn't sleep well. Got up first and found him. Still can't believe it."

I nodded. "He was a Suicide King too?"

He nodded. "Poor Danny. The Kings are active now? I haven't even thought about it in . . . a long time."

"Why'd you guys do it in the first place?" I said.

He shrugged.

"Why give other inmates a motive to kill you?" I asked. "Why—"

"We're not those kind of inmates," he said. "We were all nerds, not thugs. The only person any of us ever thought about hurting was ourselves. It was just something to do. We were bored. Brent said it'd be cool."

"You don't think nerds kill for money?"

"Not us, I'm telling you, but that was part of the fun. It was exciting—for a while, then it became boring like everything else around here and we let the whole thing drop—including the policies. Now there's no motivation."

I didn't say anything, just thought about what he had said. If the policies were no longer in effect there would be no money motive.

"I can't believe you figured out the killer's message about suicide kings from the Miguel Morales cold-case card," he said.

"If I'm right."

"I'm impressed, Chaplain. And I'm not easily impressed. Wow. You live up to the hype."

As we talked, nearly every inmate who passed us strained to hear what we were saying or asked me for something. It happened everywhere I went—Chaplain, when you gonna hook me up with a phone call? Chaplain, I need to come see you? Chaplain, help a brother out with some extra greeting cards? Chaplain, I need some extra time in the library? Chaplain, I need to come practice my music. Chaplain, Chaplain, Chaplain.

"Does the fact that the killer's leaving suicide kings

let you know who it is?"

He shook his head. "You think it's one of the club?"

"Who else?"

"But why? That was so long ago. Nothing to gain."

"Not necessarily."

"I guarantee the policies have lapsed. And if the others are like me, they'll think you can't collect if it's suicide."

"Which might be why he's leaving the cards—let us know it's not."

"Then he's risking getting caught."

"Probably figures he's too smart for that."

"Against you? He'd be crazy. I still can't get over how you—"

"Anybody outside the club know about it? Anybody have anything against the members?"

He started to shake his head, then stopped. "There was one guy who went through with it back then . . . Ralph Meeks. Think someone could be retaliating for him? Club didn't kill him, didn't do anything, but someone might blame us."

"Worth looking into."

"How long you think I'll last out here?" he asked.

"I can get you put in Protective Management or Confinement."

"As vulnerable as I am out here, I think it's safer than being locked in a cell. I know you'll figure out who the killer is. Just do it before he kills me and not after, okay?"

I was walking back to the upper compound with a list of all the members of the Suicide Kings when I ran into Hahn.

"Any thoughts on why inmates would form a suicide

club and put each other in their wills and make each other
the beneficiaries of their life insurance policies? You've
worked closely with these guys. What motivates them to do
something like that?"

"Who in particular?"

I told her.

She shook her head. "Not just one thing. A few
of them are—or were—genuinely clinically depressed.
Don't care about anything, can be talked into anything. A
few of the others are so grandiose, so . . . They truly feel
invincible."

"Like Brent Allen."

She nodded.

As usual, Hahn drew the attention of the entire
compound. A few of the caged animals made an attempt at
subtlety, but most leered and sneered and stared and ogled.
There were catcalls and lewd comments, though none quite
loud enough for us to make out what was being said or by
whom.

And as usual, I couldn't help but imagine how it
must make her feel. She didn't react, didn't respond—at
least not in any overt way they could see—but I sensed
her tensing, saw the subtle tightness in her body, the slight
awkwardness of her gait.

We walked past the last canteen and dorms and
were less than a hundred yards from the center gate. The
inmates around us thinned out, and so did the unpleasant
and unwanted attention my young, attractive coworker was
receiving.

"They're so out of touch with reality, they feel like
superheroes or something. They don't think they can die,
but if they do they think they'll transcend death, come
back somehow. Others are looking for excitement, a rush, a
high, and don't care how they get it. It's like playing Russian

Roulette. All of them are different, but nearly all of them are self-destructive in some way. It's no different from risky behavior of any kind."

Chapter Twenty-five

Jamie Lee's face lit up when she saw me, and in doing so, lit up the room. And I couldn't help but smile. She was one of the most pleasant people at the institution and was quickly becoming one of my favorite coworkers.

"Hello handsome," she said.

I turned and looked over my shoulder to make sure she was talking to me.

"Yeah, you," she said. "You get better looking every time I see you. If I were straight . . ."

"You'd still be old enough to be my mother."

"What's your point?" she said with a wicked, bare-lipped smile.

She was not a lipstick lesbian.

Jamie Lee looked like what she was—an overweight, middle-aged gay woman. She had short hair shaved in the back, a certain soft androgyny, and the build of a linebacker who'd stopped working out a decade ago.

Of course, middle-aged gay women, like middle-aged straight women, had an infinite variety of looks, and generalizing was wrong, but Jamie Lee had the look that most people associate with lesbianism, her loose-fitting green nurse uniform adding to the effect.

"I'm about to take a cancer break," she said. "Wanna

join me?"

"You bet."

We walked through the side door of Medical and out into the bright afternoon sun.

"You know what they say about second-hand smoke," she said.

"The pleasure of your company makes it worth the risk."

She carefully withdrew one of the slim cigarettes from the pack, placed it in her mouth, and lit it. After inhaling deeply with obvious pleasure, she withdrew the cigarette from her mouth and held it between her two fingers in a dainty manner.

Smoking was by far the most feminine thing she did.

Across from us the inmates assigned to inside grounds were sweeping the sidewalk and street that ran down the center of the compound. The blue uniforms the inmates wore were big and baggy and hung off them the way kids wore their jeans on the street. The plastic bags hanging from their back pockets were filled with the tiny bits of trash they had picked up, and because there were so many workers and so little trash, the bags fluttered in the breeze.

"Unfortunately, this cigarette won't last long," she said. "So . . . let the interrogation begin."

"No interrogation. Just a little chat about Danny Jacobs."

"You heard I spent a lot of time with him and wondered if I killed him?"

"I know you killed him. I want to know why."

"Danny and I were having an affair," she said. "I know it's against the rules and that I shouldn't have, but God, the rod on that man."

As she talked, she moved her hands about, the cigarette making small smoke signals in the air around them.

"You ever even seen one?"

"I'm a nurse for fuck sake," she said. "Besides, I've got a couple of special . . . ah . . . objects that look just like 'em. Or so the package said."

"I know this is gonna make me sound like one of the homophobes around here, but can I get a straight answer about Jacobs?"

"That's a hell of a thing to say to me."

I laughed.

"Okay, I've had my fun. The truth is, Dr. Alvarez asked me to watch Danny closely after he got out of the infirmary. But I would've anyway because I liked him. He was a good kid. Troubled. Tormented. But good."

"You saw him the night he died?"

"Yeah, I did. I wasn't supposed to. I mean, I'd just seen him, but he seemed really down. I thought I might cheer him up. In fact, I thought I did, but . . . I feel bad about it. It's not like we were close or anything. I just liked the kid. Sorry, but that's it. All I know. Didn't see anything suspicious, no one lurking around with a noose."

"This would be so much easier if you had."

She nodded and we were quiet a moment, but when I saw how little of her cigarette was left, I pressed on.

"What about Lance Phillips?"

"Same way," she said. "Got to know him in the infirmary. Cared for him while he recuperated."

"Danny was in Lance's bunk when he died."

"That significant?"

"If Phillips didn't try to kill himself," I said.

"You don't think he did?"

I shook my head. "I don't."

"Well, that may be true, but I was there. I saw what he tried to do. And he was in a locked confinement cell by himself. So how could someone . . . I came up shortly after it started. I saw him swinging from the rope. No one else was around. Seemed like a suicide attempt to me."

"Maybe," I said, "but if so, where'd he get the rope?"

Emile Rollins worked on an outside grounds crew cleaning and caring for the parks of Potter County. I caught up with him at the south gate as he was being patted down to reenter the institution. Unlike the other inmates around him, he stood perfectly still and kept quiet throughout the procedure. When he did move, it was in smooth, economic motions. He wasted no energy, and there was a certain fluidity to everything he did, a physical grace.

It was evening, everything lit softly. The setting sun ducking behind the slash pines to the west etched their tops with fire and ignited the horizon beyond, streaking the bottoms of the cirrus clouds with swaths of Spanish orange and salmon.

But it wasn't just the quality of light, sound too had a softness I associated with the transition of day into night.

After the officers had finished with Emile, I motioned him over and he moved toward me without hesitation or expression.

Standing before me, I could see how deceptive his build was. He was tall and thin, but very muscular. Every inch of him looked cut and ripped, pure muscle pressing out against the skin—not something easily achieved with the long muscles of a tall person.

His uniform was loose, and at a glance he looked to be anorexic, but it was an illusion. Huge veins popped out of the skin on the undersides of his forearms, and the well-defined muscles beneath them turned and twisted like steel cords as he moved his arms.

"Rollins?" I asked.

"Yes, sir."

His voice was soft and slightly higher than I expected but bore no Southern accent.

"I'd like to ask you a few questions."

"Of course."

"Tell me about Lance Phillips, Brent Allen, and Danny Jacobs."

"Whatta you wanna know? We all sleep next to each other in the dorm—or did. I knew Danny the best. Still can't believe he did it."

He looked down, but there was no sign of sadness on his face.

The officers checking in the inmates were tired and ready to go home, but the inmates were not cooperating. They were mouthing off, getting out of line, and moving slowly—seemingly on purpose, and the more the officers showed they didn't like it, the more the inmates did it.

"What about Lance? He tried to—"

"Says he didn't. I don't know. You can never tell with Lance, he probably just wanted to get out of Confinement, but I thought Danny was doing good—well, good for him."

"Do you know of anyone who would want to hurt either of them?" I asked.

He shook his head.

"You a member of their club?"

"What club? Gunners?"

Gunners were inmates who masturbated in front of female officers.

"Suicide Kings."

"Don't think so. They may've made me an honorary

member or something 'cause we hang out, but I told 'em I ain't ever gonna kill myself."

I nodded. "What can you tell me about Danny's death?"

"Nothing," he said. "Just a normal night. We all went to bed. When we woke up he was dead."

He said it with no feeling. Just stating the facts. Perhaps like so many of the men in here, he was incapable of attachment. Or maybe all associations inside were ones of need and convenience, and didn't involve anything like empathy.

"Anybody out of the ordinary in the dorm that night?"

"It'd be quicker to tell you who wasn't there. We had more traffic than we've ever had before. By a long shot. A nurse came by. And the doctor, but not at the same time."

"Baldwin?" I asked.

"She was there too, at some point, but I was talking about the medical doctor."

"*Alvarez*?"

He nodded. "And the psych lady."

"You already said her."

"Not Dr. Baldwin. That other one. What's her name?"

"Ling?"

"Yeah. Small, black-haired Asian chick. They all talked to Danny. Every one of 'em. All at different times. All pretty late. Before lights out, but . . ."

The officers finished checking the inmates in and they all began to move toward the internal gate of the sally port to be buzzed back in to their dorms.

We fell in line with the others and walked through the gate after it was buzzed open by the officer in the tower.

He shook his head. "People thinking I'm a Suicide King mean I'm in danger?"

The large gate rolled back into place, clanging loudly as it reached the other side. Everyone was locked in again. Another day without an escape.

It was dark now, the only light coming from a street lamp near the maintenance building on the other side of the fence and a flood light shining down into the sally port from one of the tall poles supporting the south gate.

"You think of any reason someone would want to kill the Kings?"

"No," he said. "I can't."

"Well, I'd keep thinking about it, I were you. Might turn out to be valuable information one day."

Chapter Twenty-six

"**Y**ou didn't tell me you were in A-dorm the night Danny died."

Across the table from me Hahn stiffened, then sat perfectly still for a moment.

She had come to my office to go over the list of Suicide Kings and tell me what she knew about each one.

"I didn't?" she asked.

"Why didn't you?"

She shrugged. "It never came up, I guess. I'm not sure."

"I can't believe you didn't mention it."

"You don't suspect me, do you?"

"Of what?"

"I don't know. I just . . . I'm sorry I didn't say anything sooner."

"*Sooner*? You didn't say anything at all. *I* brought it up, remember? You don't think that's a little suspicious?"

"I think you've been around criminals too long. The only suspicious thing is your mind. What's so odd about me visiting A-dorm?"

"You don't do it that often, it was at night so you were off, and it just happened to be the night someone was killed down there."

"Can we talk about something else?" she said. "*Seriously?*"

"There's nothing to tell . . . and I have information for you that might actually help you figure out who's doing it."

I shook my head, but she looked down at her notes and pressed on.

"Of the original Suicide Kings, only three are left inside—Lance Phillips, Brent Allen, and Emile Rollins. One, Myer Goodis, finished his sentence and now lives in Fort Walton Beach. And two are dead—Danny Jacobs and Ralph Meeks. According to everything official, they both committed suicide. Everyone I spoke to says there was nothing suspicious about Meek's death. It was definitely suicide."

"How long ago did—"

"Nearly two years. Hard to see it having anything to do with what's going on now."

I nodded.

"What *is* going on now?" she asked.

I shrugged.

It was evening, just minutes after the end of our work day, and we were at a little convenience store not far from the prison.

In addition to the normal beer, gas, junk food, and lottery tickets, the small store had a deli that served fried chicken, pizza, and hot wings—all of it as bad as any I had ever tried.

There were two booth-style tables in the back corner not far from the deli. We were in one of them. No one was in the other.

White ceramic cups of coffee in saucers sat in front of us on the table but Hahn was the only one actually drinking any.

The only person on duty, a middle-aged woman with red fro-ish hair was behind the counter, her attention focused on her phone.

"You think someone's trying to kill all the remaining Suicide Kings or just Lance and Danny? Or just Lance? Did Danny kill himself?"

"The ones that are left, what are they in for?"

"Drugs or drug-related robbery for Jacobs and Rollins. Phillips, conspiracy and fraud. Allen for manslaughter."

"Who'd he kill?"

"Sister. There's family money—both were due to inherit. Now, just him. It was a boating accident. Prosecutor suspected murder, could only get criminal negligence. Allen had been drinking. Says he didn't mean to kill her."

"Whatta you think?"

"I think he did."

I nodded. "What about the staff members in the dorm? Anything come up?"

"Dr. Alvarez has had some trouble on the street. Malpractice stuff. All the cases settled with his insurance, so no convictions, but he doesn't practice anywhere but here."

"They don't really care who does the doctoring on inmates, do they?"

She smirked, raised her eyebrows, and tilted her head. "Just a position that has to be filled. Not many successful doctors lining up to work inside."

"Is the same true of us? We inside because we failed or ran into trouble on the street?"

"True of a lot of people who work inside, not all. Some of us just live in a small area without a lot of opportunity. Doctor can make a lot more money outside. Same's not true for a minister or nurse or counselor."

I nodded.

"Though Alvarez is making money—lots of it. He can't practice—or doesn't, but he owns a clinic."

"Interesting."

"Baldwin's clean—legal-wise, anyway. She does have constant man trouble. So many neuroses, so much drama. Donnie Foster's clean. So's Jamie Lee."

"What about you?"

She didn't say anything.

She wasn't on the list because I didn't know she was down there, but—

I abandoned the thought as a young Hispanic man in a black cowboy getup walked in carrying a gun.

Chapter Twenty-seven

The small bell above the door had not even caused Red to look up, and I hoped she would remain oblivious for whatever happened next.

He scanned the store slowly until his eyes came to rest on me.

I waited.

With no weapon and two women in close proximity, I didn't have a lot of options.

He moved toward me and Hahn, which meant he was moving away from Red and the cash register.

He wasn't here to rob the place.

"You Jordan?" he asked.

He wore black jeans, black cowboy boots, and a long-sleeve black button-down shirt. A white vest with black stitched designs was open to reveal a horse-head bolero at the top and matching belt buckle at the bottom.

"Yeah," I said. "Not the basketball player, the nobody."

He smiled. "Only one M.J."

"King of pop might not agree," I said.

He nodded very slowly as he seemed to consider what I had said with far more earnestness than it was worthy of.

"True," he said. "Very true, señor."

"You consider everything that carefully?" I said.

He seemed to consider that.

"*Seriously*?" I said.

He sat down across from me and next to Hahn, but didn't acknowledge her in any way. She slid over as far as she could.

He leveled the .45 at me, but I only saw it in my peripheral vision. My eyes didn't leave his.

The pungent odor pouring from his pores mixed with the scent of what I recognized to be a popular body spray. The unpleasant alchemical affect was one of aging ethnic food and drugstore deodorizer roasting in a hot car.

The body spray was advertised to drive women wild. So far Hahn had somehow found the strength to resist.

"Pretty calm," he said. "That come from spending so much time with guys like me?"

"What kind of guy is that?"

"Type does what needs to be done, amigo—sometimes for other people."

"Oh," I said. "An errand boy."

He smiled. "Been called worse."

"I bet."

Hahn was obviously scared, but she was holding her own just fine.

Without acknowledging her, he lifted her coffee cup and drank from it, wincing as he did.

"That is very bad, jefe," he said.

"Everything here is," I said. "It's sort of their thing."

"Somebody needs to shoot the clown behind the counter," he said.

I looked over at Red, who was still unaware that anything was going on, then back at the cowboy.

"So what errand brings you to this joint? Chicken, pizza, beer?"

"You," he said. "I am here for you, jefe. I have been asked to gently remind you that you are a chaplain not a . . . Just mind your own business and not that of others. Only trouble for you in it."

"Others and trouble are my business," I said.

"This is just a warning," he said. "But you only get one."

"Then could you be a little more specific?" I said. "I got a lot goin' on right now. It'd be embarrassing if I got killed for stopping the wrong thing."

"Let us just say it involves issues of life and death, which is a good thing for you to remember."

When he glanced back at Red, his eyes came alive for the first time. "Goddamn, but I like gringo redheads." He glanced back at Hahn. "I mean no offense, señorita."

"You delivered your message," I said. "Any particular reason you're still here?"

He seemed to contemplate that for a long moment, rubbing a thumbnail against his smooth jawline as he did.

"You see this?" he said, lifting the gun. "This lets me do whatever I want. Stay where I want for as long as I want."

He held the gun like they did in the movies.

"You ever shot anyone?" I asked.

He didn't respond.

"It's harder than it looks," I said. "Even at a target, but especially at a living human being. And to kill a man. It's like nothing you've ever known."

"The hell kind of preacher are you?"

"The convict kind," I said. "But I wasn't always that."

He nodded appreciatively. "Explains a lot. Well . . . is

what it is. Just remember what I said. Okay, amigo?"

He stood and moved away quickly. A moment later, he was out the door, the small bell jingling causing Red to look up for the first time.

"You okay?" I asked.

Hahn nodded.

"Sorry about all that."

She shook her head. "It's okay."

Without thinking, she started to take a sip of her coffee, but I stopped her.

"His prints are on your cup," I said. "Safe money says he's got a record."

Chapter Twenty-eight

"If he Hispanic," Merrill said, "possible he connected to Miguel Morales? Like maybe it *was* about him?"

We were standing in front of the convenience store in the nearly empty parking lot.

"Could be," I said. I hadn't considered it, but I should have. "Couldn't find a connection between him and Lance but . . ."

"What about the other Kings?"

"Didn't even know they existed at the time," I said. "Need to find out now we do."

The night was dark and damp, grayish clouds intermittently obscuring a small wedge of moon.

Hahn had gone home. Red remained oblivious.

In my right hand was a paper bag with the coffee cup the gunman had touched in it.

Hahn had been shaken up when she left, but she was more angry at my persistence in asking what she was doing in Danny's dorm the night he was killed, than anything else.

Driving home later, my phone rang.

"Hey."

It took me a moment to place the soft, sad voice. It

was Cheryl Jacobs.

"Hey. How are you? I was going to call to check on you, but—"

"I'm struggling. Would you mind . . . I mean . . . Is there any way . . . Could I talk to you for a few minutes?"

"Of course."

"Sorry to be a bother."

"Absolutely no bother at all."

"Nights are the worst. I do okay during the day. Get through. But . . . when the sun sinks . . . so do I."

"I understand," I said. "I've been there."

"I have no one now. There's . . . no one. A mother's supposed to die before her son. He's supposed to be at my funeral with his wife and kids there to comfort him, supposed to console himself that I had a long life, that it's the natural order of things."

I wasn't so sure the natural order of things helped all that much. I thought about Mom, about how difficult I was finding her imminent death.

Thou know'st 'tis common; all that live must die. You must know that your father lost a father. That father lost, lost his.

A hollow argument. At least Hamlet found it so.

Convention, tradition, the natural order of things offer little consolation in the devastating face of deep grief.

I nodded, though she couldn't see me, and continued listening, and I was struck by how much of my life I spent doing those two things. Nodding and listening. Listening and nodding. Wasn't much else to do most of the time— particularly in situations like this.

"In my entire life I've never wanted to die before," she said.

"You do now?"

"I do," she said, and paused for a moment before

continuing, letting her words hang there in the dark, damp night between us. "Don't worry, I'm not . . . I don't mean . . . I'm not really considering it. I've just never even had the feeling before."

"I understand."

"You ever felt like killing yourself?"

"I've never had that exact feeling, no."

"I now understand a little better what Danny went through. I couldn't at the time. And I couldn't do anything for him. Just got him a good counselor and kept loving him."

"How many actual attempts did he make?"

"A few. Not sure exactly. Some may've been accidents . . . or . . . I don't really know. But he got better, got past all that, and . . . I just hope he didn't sink back down into . . . You don't think he did, do you?"

"I don't."

"It's so cruel . . . I mean if someone made it look like . . . they must've known he had been . . . You're so easy to talk to, so nonjudgemental and understanding. I feel like I can tell you anything."

"You can."

"I feel like such a failure as a mom. Everyone else has always thought that. This is the first time *I* have."

"Why do you?"

"I don't know. I guess . . . even if he was murdered . . . he wouldn't have been in prison if it weren't for . . ."

"Addiction," I said. "My mother *is* an addict—or was, but she's not responsible for my addiction."

"Yours?"

I nodded.

"But you're—"

"In recovery . . . It's far less of an issue in my life now, but I'll always be an addict—and that's not my mom's or anyone else's fault."

"Thanks. Thank you. Could you . . ." she began, then trailed off. "You think you could . . . Would you mind helping me with Danny's memorial service?"

"Of course. I'd be honored."

"You're kind of all I've got right now."

Chapter Twenty-nine

"Everybody's a whore," Carla Jean said. "I'm just honest about it. Don't get me wrong, I ain't no street walker. Not some Meth Head Mandy, do anything for a fix. Just keepin' it real by sayin' I get paid for services rendered like any other job."

We were at a mostly empty no-name bar just outside the city limits.

It was late.

I was at the end of the bar, a Dr. Pepper with grenadine in front of me. Carla Jean, who was the weeknight bartender, was behind the bar, leaning in toward me as we talked, her braless breasts pressing against the countertop.

People referred to Carla Jean Columbus as the town's most brazen whore, but I found her unapologetic truthfulness refreshing. I just wondered if her brazenness was born of self-acceptance and peace or defensiveness and self-delusion.

"Everything comes down to money," she said. "Everything. It's how the world works. What are we willing to do for money. Well guess what. I'm willing to fuck for money. I like to fuck. I'm gettin' paid to do something I like. And I don't do it if I don't want to. I don't do anything

I don't want to."

"You say who and you say when . . . and you say who," I said in my best Julia Roberts.

She looked confused. "Huh?"

"Line from *Pretty Woman*."

"Oh."

At the opposite end of the bar, a distance that seemed worlds away, an extremely wrinkled old lady with a faded pink golfer's hat on and a middle-aged man in a blue mechanic uniform sat next to each other drinking alone.

"What can you tell me about that night at the farmhouse?"

She couldn't tell me much. It was the same as all the rest. Men taking turns with her, mostly good guys, an occasional asshole, easiest money she'd made in months.

"Did you know the blonde girl?"

"The one that got killed? No. Least I don't think so. Who was she?"

"That's what I'm tryin' to find out," I said. "That and what happened to her."

"I didn't even see her," she said. "Didn't know she was there 'til y'all showed up askin' questions about her."

"I thought you let her in."

"Let her in what? It's not my club."

"The farmhouse. I was told you let her in the back door."

"Well I don't know who told you that but I didn't let anybody in. And I didn't see no blonde girl."

"You didn't let her inside? You sure?"

"Positive. I didn't let anyone in at any time the whole time we were there."

I thought about what it meant that Carla Jean hadn't

let the victim inside and how it impacted the inquiry.

"So you have no idea who she was or why she was there?" I asked.

"My guess . . . she was crashin'," she said. "Bet you anything. Tryin' to make a buck, tryin' to take money out of my pocket. She heard about the party and figured she could sneak in on our action. That or someone brought her. Decided he'd pimp her out to those horny old bastards."

Maybe someone really did bring her to embarrass or even blackmail one or more of the men running for office. Maybe Dad wasn't paranoid, just political.

"Still can't believe she was killed," she said. "I mean, fuck. Am I in danger?"

I fell asleep beside Anna later that night thinking about the blonde—wondering who she was, why she was there, why she was killed, why her body was staged next to the prison fence, and why her body would then be stolen on its way to the morgue.

If she never entered the farmhouse what did that change? The suspects? Those with means and opportunity?

I woke up a little while later, mind racing.

Placing my hand on Anna's bare thigh, I laid there in the dark, listening to her breathing, observing the thoughts ricocheting around inside me.

Two murders.

One premeditated. The other impromptu.

Is that right?

Two murderers.

One patient. The other impulsive.

One plots and plans, watches and waits. The other snaps, acts, reacts, lashes out, explodes.

Is one killer mature and the other juvenile? Or does

it have more to do with the means, motive, and opportunity than the makeup of the man?

Any of this true? Does it fit the facts, the actions of the killers, the circumstances of the cases? If so, what does it say about them?

Who are these figures I can't quite make out? What did they unwittingly reveal about themselves? What signature did they leave? What clues?

What do they want? Why did they do it? Greed? Lust? Envy? Psychopathology? Fear of being found out? For what?

Will either of them do it again? What's the key to catching them?

What do their victims reveal about them? I know so little about the ones and next to nothing about the other.

Need more info.

Do you? What if you don't? What if you already know everything you need to?

Do I?

I awoke the next morning with no insights or answers.

Over breakfast Anna said, "Stealing the body hides her identity and effectively makes it impossible to catch the killer."

I nodded. "I don't disagree, but why not just do that from the beginning? Take the body and hide it or dispose of it right after you commit the murder—like many murderers do? Why take the time to load it up, take it to the prison, lean it against the fence, risk being seen or caught, just to steal it a few hours later?"

Chapter Thirty

"**S**omebody killing Suicide Kings or just trying to off Phillips?" Merrill asked.

"Not sure. Danny *was* in Lance's bunk," I said. "So . . ."

"Why?"

"Liked the mattress better. It's thicker or something. Felt safer in the top bunk."

Merrill shook his head.

It was the next morning. We were standing near the internal gate. Inmates were going to and from breakfast at the chow hall. Most of them were quiet in the coolness of the early morning, moving sleepily through a routine as rote as dressing, but some were already mouthy—miserable and anxious to spread it around.

"Some these bitches wake up lookin' for a fight," Merrill said.

"Not something they can sleep off," I said.

We were quiet a moment, continuing to watch the long lines of wasting potential. Whatever their lives had been before, whatever they would be again, at the moment, they were on pause, prison a parenthetical in their existence like a drunk's weekend blackout—except when they woke up from this they'd remember every brutal detail.

"You get the Confinement log from the night of the

attempt on Lance?" I asked.

He tossed two sheets of paper toward me and they drifted down into my hand. The top one was a copy of all staff members and officers who visited Confinement that night.

I pulled a pen out of my coat pocket and circled the names of those who'd also made an appearance in A-dorm the night Jacobs was killed.

"Usual suspects?" he said.

"Those in Confinement when the attempt was made on Lance and in A-dorm when Danny was killed are Jamie Lee, Bailey Baldwin, Dr. Juan Alvarez, Donnie Foster, Mark Lawson, and . . ."

"And?"

"Hahn Ling."

He smiled. "You know how to pick 'em."

"Pick 'em? We had a few dates—and that's been a while. And only because the one I really picked wasn't available yet."

"Is now, ain't she?"

I smiled.

"How's it going with you two?"

"Before we got together I had an unrealistic expectation of what it would be like, a fantasy, a dream of perfection."

He nodded.

"It's a billion times better than that," I added.

He smiled. "Happy for you. Y'all both deserve it."

"Thanks."

"What about inmates who were at both?"

I looked at the second sheet.

When my eyes grew wide, he said, "What?"

"Danny was in Confinement the night the attempt

was made on Lance."

"Doing what?"

"Passing out food trays," I said.

"No way he got in his cell, but . . . be a hell of a coincidence if it just a coincidence."

I nodded without looking up from the logs.

"Brent Allen was also there," I said.

"Motherfucker can't kill his own rat ass, but he can kill his friends?"

The captain on duty standing near the food service building called one of the inmates out of the chow line and began to yell at him about needing to shave. The inmate claimed to have a shaving pass, but couldn't produce it. The captain sent him back to the dorm without any breakfast.

"Allen was actually in Confinement," I said. "Got out the next day."

"The plot thickens."

"It gets even thicker. He was in the cell next to Lance."

"And he didn't mention it to you?"

I shook my head. "Lot of that going on."

He smiled. "'Course, bein' in the next confinement cell like being in the next state. Not like he could do anything."

"Not without help."

"You think maybe the cell defective?"

"Worth checking out," I said. "Thanks."

Lance Phillips waved at us as he passed by in the line of inmates heading for the chow hall. I waved back. Merrill did not.

Merrill cleared his throat as a slight flicker appeared in his eyes, and I slid the copies of the logs into the pocket of my coat. When I turned around, I saw Mark Lawson approaching us.

"Chaplain," he said as he walked up. "Lot of people 'round here say what a good man you are, but I keep on hearing you're asking questions about my investigation. I don't wanna get off on the wrong foot, but seems like that's what's happenin'."

"I've been asking a few questions," I said, "but not about the way you're investigating."

Lawson's white short-sleeve shirt, clip-on tie, and gray cotton pants were wrinkled, a size too small, and his pea-green prison tattoos glowed in the morning sun.

"I don't mean about me as an investigator," he said, stepping forward, putting his face a little too close to mine. "I mean you been conducting your own investigation."

I nodded.

"Well, don't. This is my first big investigation here and I don't want the integrity of it compromised."

"I won't get in your investigation," I said. "And I won't get in your way, but I will continue to ask questions. And if I come across anything that might be helpful, I'll pass it along."

"No," he said, shaking his head. "I've already talked to the warden. If I have to, I'll go to the regional director."

He then turned and walked away.

I saw Lance Phillips come out of the chow hall and start to approach us, but when he saw Lawson standing nearby, he turned and went back in.

"Nobody want you workin' this thing, do they?" Merrill said. "Almost as if they's somethin' at stake and they have somethin' to hide or protect. Speakin' of . . . seen the Hispanic cowboy again?" Merrill asked.

I shook my head.

"Hope I'm around the next time he ride into town."

"Dad's running his prints," I said. "Maybe we'll ride

into his."

"Even better."

Chapter Thirty-one

After leaving Merrill, I walked over to Confinement and asked to inspect the cells Phillips and Allen occupied the night of Lance's supposed suicide attempt.

I was told by the nervous young officer that he didn't have the authority for anything like that.

There were inmates in both cells, and it would've been a hassle to cuff them, pull them, and place them in other cells while I had my little look around—which, I suspected, was the real reason he wasn't willing.

"Why not get the warden, colonel, or inspector to do it?" he asked. "Seems more like their job anyway. But, truth is, I can save you the trouble. We done inspections of both cells and there ain't a thing in the world wrong with either of 'em."

Back in my office, I made a few calls about the life insurance policies taken out by the Suicide Kings. Each was designed to pay in cases of suicide after two years, but they had all long since lapsed for nonpayment. Because Ralph Meeks's death had been ruled a suicide and because it was less than two years since the policy had been taken out, the company, Florida Farm Mutual, had refused to pay, instead refunding the price of the premiums.

Lapsed policies meant no money motive. And would make it far, far more challenging to find out what was going on and why.

Next, I checked their general financial situations.

In addition to having been each other's life insurance beneficiaries, the Kings were also in each other's wills, but as all of them were destitute, that too provided no motive or insight.

Next, I attempted to obtain information about Ralph Meeks's death, but after several calls found nothing helpful. Everyone involved treated it like a suicide, so even if there had been evidence to the contrary, it had gone unnoticed, unrecognized, unrecorded.

According to those involved, there was nothing suspicious, no signs of foul play, and no playing cards on his person or in his property.

Every investigation had dead-ends, and you never knew what they would be until you reached them. Over the years, I had followed far more than my fair share of them, so I was used to them, part of the process, but that didn't make them any less frustrating.

I took a deep breath, rolled my shoulders, and was about to call Dad when my phone rang.

It was Dad.

"I was just about to call you," I said.

"How are you?"

"Okay. How about you?"

"Can't complain."

We were quiet for a moment.

"I was calling to thank you," he said.

"For?"

"All that you do for your mom."

I instantly felt guilty for how little I had done recently.

"I went by to see her this morning," he said. "It's obvious you're helping her in so many ways. And I really appreciate it."

Even after being divorced longer than they were married, Dad kept tabs on Mom, mostly through me. Since she'd gotten sick and sober, he'd done it more directly.

"I should do more. Haven't done even what I normally do lately."

"You're doing a lot—and not just for her."

I didn't say anything, and we were quiet another moment.

Dad and I were so different, our relationship so pragmatic—like everything in his life—that it was often awkward between us.

"Well," he said, "that's all I wanted to say."

"Thanks."

"You were about to call me," he said. "What'd you need?"

"Wondered if you were makin' any progress on the case?"

"Not a lick," he said. "Town talk is it's the nail in my coffin. It *is* embarrassing. And I can't figure it out to save my life—my political one anyway. Did you read the paper this morning? If it's not about making me look bad, hell, if it's not about making all of us lose our damn jobs, I don't know what it could be."

"Maybe it is," I said. "I think we need to consider that as a real possibility."

"So take a closer look at Hugh," he said. "But I do that and it just looks like I'm playing politics, trying to bully him out of the race."

"I'll see what I can do," I said.

"Thanks. I really do think this thing could cost all of us our jobs. Me and Judge Cox for sure. Stockton is safe. Not sure about Ralph."

"I talked to Carla Jean last night," I said. "She says she never let the victim in the house."

"You believe her?"

"I'm inclined to."

"What does it mean if she didn't? How does that change anything as far as what might have happened? This thing is going to make me lose my mind."

"We'll figure it out," I said. "Hang in there. Hey, the inmate I told you about who supposedly committed suicide . . . Interim inspector's shutting me out of the investigation. Think you could find out what the ME's report says?"

"I'll do what I can."

Chapter Thirty-two

Hahn's small frame was wrapped up in a black cropped cable sweater, her narrow hips in a loose-fitting black skirt with a draw-string waist, which reached down to black lace-up boots. The skirt was shiny like her hair, and her outfit and complexion made her dark, dazzling eyes pop all the more.

We were walking through the pine forest toward the small pond between the prison and Potter Farm on our lunch break, the tall slash pines above us giving way to shorter pond pines and finally to cypress trees as we drew closer to the water's edge.

Hahn moved like she did everything, with energy and enthusiasm, often jumping out in front of me, turning to face me as we walked.

"Ready to hear my confession?"

I nodded. "Why now and not before?"

She shrugged. "It felt like such betrayal. Still does, but I don't . . . I know you'll . . . I trust you."

I wasn't sure I believed her, but I nodded and smiled as if I did.

"Father forgive me for I have sinned. It's been forever since my last confession . . ."

The grass beneath our feet was still mostly green,

thick like expensive carpet, and white and gold flowers were sprinkled throughout the thick foliage on either side of the path.

"I went down to A-dorm the night Danny Jacobs was killed to check on him."

"Because . . ."

"I was worried about him."

"Why?"

"I'm not sure exactly. It was just a feeling—and it was right."

I nodded. "Yes it was."

"I can't really explain it, but . . . I just think something's going on in Medical. Something not right. And don't ask . . . it's just a lot of little things. I wouldn't even mention this to someone else. And all the boys on your list have been in and out of there a lot lately."

"The Suicide Kings?"

"Yeah," she said. "I'm not sure what it is . . . but, well, I probably shouldn't say anything until I know something."

"If you can't tell me what you know, tell me what you feel."

She stopped walking, and we stood there for a moment in the middle of the quiet forest beneath the thin pines.

Finally, she shook her head. "It's just off. Something's going on that's not . . ."

She started walking again, and I followed.

When we reached the pond, we paused to take in its beauty. The small body of water sat in the bowl of gentle slope, rimmed by cypress trees, surrounded by pine flats on every side.

I breathed in deeply, taking it in.

We walked down to the edge of the pond and sat down on a thick pad of grass.

"I can narrow it down a bit," she said. "It's not all of Medical. It's . . . Dr. Alvarez and . . ."

"And?"

"Dr. Baldwin."

I nodded.

"She's my supervisor, and I like her. I really do, but when she's around him . . . I don't know . . ."

"They were both in the dorm the night Jacobs was killed," I said.

"I know."

"And in Confinement the night Lance was supposed to have attempted suicide."

"So was I."

"I know."

The midday sun shimmered on the still surface of the small pond. Spanish moss draped across the branches of the cypress trees surrounding it, waving in the wind like fresh laundry on the line.

"I'd have Bailey help me unlock it if she wasn't one of the ones making me feel so—"

"Unlock it?"

"Unpack it. You know. Help me think it through. Maybe even use hypnotherapy."

"Hypnotherapy?"

"She does it a lot. She's very good at it. She's taught me so much."

"You do it too?"

"I'm just learning."

I thought about it for a moment, and she let me.

"If someone were suicidal—or had been—could you use hypnotherapy to give them a little nudge?"

"You could suggest it, but I don't think it would—"

"What is it?"

"She'd been using it on Danny, supposedly for addiction recov— Oh, my God."

"What?"

"That night. I . . . I was across the dorm, so I can't be sure. I couldn't hear them, but . . ."

"But what?"

"It looked like she was hypnotizing him."

I leaned in toward her, energy jangling through me.

"Maybe if he was already suicidal, she could've gotten him to do it when she wasn't there."

"And," I added, "gotten Lance Phillips to do it inside a locked cell."

Merrill and I found Baldwin and Alvarez together in his office.

They stopped talking abruptly when we walked in, and didn't offer us a seat.

"I was just leaving," Baldwin said. "I'll let you all talk."

Merrill moved in front of the door.

"We came to see *you*," I said, "but we'd like to talk to both of you."

She glared at Merrill, then looked at Alvarez for support, but found none. Finally, she sat down again. "What's this about?"

"Hypnosis, Confinement visits, murder."

"*Murder*? I thought he committed suicide."

"Who?"

"Don't play games with me, Chaplain. We all know you mean Danny Jacobs."

"What has that got to do with us?" Alvarez said.

They were the first words he had spoken, and they

came out in a heavily accented rhythm uncommon to
English.

"That what we want to know," Merrill said.

"What?" Baldwin said in outrage, but it lacked
conviction.

"We're talking to everyone who was in the dorm the
night Jacobs was killed and in Confinement the night the
attempt was made on Lance Phillips. You two were in both
places."

"One cannot practice medicine from a desk,"
Alvarez said. "I—how do you say it?—make the house call.
I am very dedicated to my medicine. I make the rounds
constantly."

Juan Alvarez was a middle-aged Hispanic man with
a light complexion and coarse, black hair going gray. He
wasn't fat exactly, but overweight, soft, fleshy. His eyes
protruded out of his head, as if too much was stuffed into
his skull, and when he widened them, which was often, they
seemed to pop out.

"You *do*," Bailey said to him. Then to us, "He does."

"But what were you doing in those particular places
at those particular times?"

"Checking on patients I had discharged from the
infirmary," he said. "My care of them does not end when
they walk out of this building."

"Same thing with me," Baldwin said. "I keep telling
Hahn if you want to be effective, you've got to go where
the patients are. Meet them on their turf, in their world. It's
amazing what that can teach you about their needs. Know
what I mean?"

"You know what she mean?" Merrill asked.

I shrugged.

"So y'all's just down there checkin' on patients," he
added. "Doing no harm, shit like that?"

"Yes."

"Eleven-thirty at night?" Merrill said. "Get the fuck outta here."

"It is true," Alvarez said. "We are very dedicated. Our patients are our lives. We practice giving help because we want to help others, we want to make a difference in the world."

"Do you have any other patients?"

"What?"

"Do either of you practice medicine or psychiatry anywhere else?" I asked.

Bailey looked at Alvarez.

"No," Alvarez said. "I am a physician for the state of Florida only. That is all. Florida has been very good to me. I love America. I own many things. Rental property. Clinic. Restaurant. But the only patients I have are here. In here I am doctor. Out there I am businessman."

"Do either of you have any idea who might have tried to kill Lance?" I asked.

They both shook their heads.

Baldwin said, "I'd look at those Suicide Kings."

"You know about them?"

"Well . . . yeah. And they're bonkers."

"*Bonkers?*"

Merrill said, "Can you put that in terms we can understand? Just speak English." He looked at Alvarez. "No offense."

Alvarez didn't get it, just shook his head in confusion and gave a small smile.

"Sorry we could not help more," Alvarez said. "But we really must return to work now. If we think of anything other we call you."

Ignoring him, I looked at Baldwin. "Whatta you use hypnotherapy for?"

She winced and shuttered slightly, but recovered quickly. "Ah, well, all sorts of things—treatment of pain, depression, anxiety, phobias, stress, habit disorders, gastro-intestinal disorders, skin conditions, post—all sorts of things. Why?"

"Ever use it on Lance or Danny?"

"Not as I recall, but I may have. I use it on all my patients."

"They were your patients, weren't they?"

"Lance still is."

"So you've used it on them."

"Oh, well, yes. I thought you meant . . . Yes, I guess I have."

Chapter Thirty-three

Passing through the waiting room for Medical, Classification, and Psychology on my way to Hahn's office, the desk sergeant held up the phone. "For you."

"Thanks," I said as I took it from him.

"I'm not supposed to be talking to you about this."

It took me a minute, but I recognized the voice as that of Hank Sproul, the forensic pathologist who had performed the autopsy on Danny Jacobs.

"I realize that," I said. "And I really appreciate it."

"I'm doing it for your dad. He's good people. I owe him. Just keep it between us."

The waiting room was overflowing with hostile inmates seeking relief from the state workers behind the two locked doors on either side of the room. Many of them suffered from paranoia and narcissism and a sense of victimhood that their daily interactions with the mammoth immovable machine of the DOC only served to confirm.

"I found nothing to contradict it was anything but self-strangulation."

I thought about it.

"However, since there was no note and this method is very rarely used in suicide . . ."

"It could be murder?"

"I can't say that. I checked everything very carefully. When your dad called, I checked everything again."

"Can you say it wasn't murder?"

"Not definitively."

"Anything you can't account for?" I said. "Anything at all?"

He hesitated and there was nothing but static on the line for a long moment.

"Only one thing," he said slowly. "There's usually way more than that. This was a very clean death and autopsy. There were some small pinpricks on the decedent's left hand fingertips."

I waited to see if more was coming.

"They were very small. Probably nothing at all, but I can't account for them."

"Like from a needle? Was he drugged?"

"Tox tests didn't reveal any drugs in his system."

"But that's the kind of punctures we're talking about. Like from a needle or—"

"Yeah. They would've been easy to miss. I'm surprised I discovered them."

"Could they be where drops of blood were drawn, like for a slide?"

"Possibly."

"What about from checking his blood sugar levels?"

"Sure. Something like that," he said. "Except he wasn't a diabetic."

"You got a book on hypnotherapy?"

"Several," Hahn said.

"I need a textbook-type definition of what hypnotherapy is used for."

"Why?"

"Something Baldwin said—well, stopped herself from saying."

"You don't need a book, you've got me. Hypnotherapy is used to treat pain, depression, anxiety, stress, phobias, hemophilia, skin conditions, post-surgical recovery, relief of—"

"That's it."

"That's what?"

"What she stopped herself from saying."

"What?"

"Post-surgical recovery."

"Really? That's interesting."

"You mind walking me through exactly how hypnotherapy works?"

"I can do better than that," she said. "I can give you a demonstration."

"I want you to be comfortable," Hahn said in a slow, soft, monotonous voice. "Adjust your clothes, your shoes, the way you're sitting, so you can be free and comfortable."

The inmate in the seat in front of her, a small, pale boy with fine blond hair, began to move his limbs and wiggle into his chair just a little more in an attempt to be comfortable and free.

"Now, as we begin, you're going to be aware that we're in a professional environment and that we're being watched, but as you relax, there is no need for the things surrounding us to have any impact on this process."

He nodded, his head and eyelids already seeming relaxed and heavy.

"I'm going to ask you to look up, fixing your gaze on a particular spot that you are comfortable with, okay?"

He nodded and began to stare at a picture of Freud on the wall behind Hahn.

"Found one?"

He nodded.

"Once you've fixed your eyes on it, don't turn away from it. Keep your head in that position so that your ears'll remain still and you'll be able to hear the various inflections and intonations of my voice. That'll enable you to better focus on what we're doing."

Hahn paused, but he didn't respond in any way I could observe.

"Don't worry about your thoughts," she continued. "There will be many racing through your head. You might wonder, 'Am I doing this right?' or 'What does she mean?' Nothing is wrong. Everything is right. Everything. Okay? Don't waste time trying to play a role you think you're supposed to or doing what you've done before. Just relax, be comfortable, and be yourself."

Hahn's office was warmer than usual, and I wondered if that had anything to do with the hypnotic process. It might not have, but the heat and the continual monotonous sound of her voice were making *me* sleepy.

"Now, you'll notice that your eyes will blink from time to time," she continued, her voice droning on like a recording. "It's a very natural thing. It's a protective mechanism because the eyes weren't designed to maintain a fixed stare. When it happens, feel comfortable about it. Your eyes will also tear. It's a normal reaction to your eyes' fixed state. It's okay. Everything is okay. The object you're staring at may distort occasionally. That's natural too, so expect that to happen. Let it happen. It's okay. Everything is okay. And finally, your eyes will grow heavy and want to close. It's the same thing that happens when you read or watch TV. When it happens, let it. Let them naturally close, and then feel how you can seem to funnel back into the privacy of yourself."

His eyes were beginning to blink more frequently and then close, only opening occasionally.

"That's it," she said. "You're doing great. I notice that you are already relaxing. That's fine. You're doing fine. You'll notice that you're beginning to feel much more comfortable. Your eyes are more comfortable closed than open. Just relax and be comfortable. You're doing great."

She paused for a moment, then continued.

"Now if you take a deep breath and let it go, you'll find you're descending into the realm of relaxation . . . each muscle letting go, so that you feel limp like a rag doll. Take whatever number of deep breaths you need, letting them out slowly. Feel yourself descend, level by level, descend until you arrive at the place where you need to be for us to accomplish what we're here to accomplish."

It looked to me like he had already arrived at that place. His whole body had changed, relaxing in on itself somehow, and he was sitting like he might if he were alone, but not how he would had he been aware of our presence in the room.

His eyes were already closed. He was already under. If hypnotism was being used for destructive purposes, then inmates like this one were sheep to the slaughter.

". . . off the merry-go-round," Hahn was saying. She never stopped talking during this process. "This is the first time your mind doesn't have to act like an executive in making all your decisions, in resolving all your concerns. Now, feel the sensation as if every cell, every organ, every system in your body is being rejuvenated. Reborn."

I realized that Hahn and the inmate had become my fixed objects and I was about to go under. I shook my head and looked away. Being hypnotized came far more easy than I would've thought.

". . . gather all the physical discomfort and tension, and imagine putting it on your shoulders and then having God lift it off. Doesn't that feel wonderful? Aren't you lighter, more relaxed? Now, as I continue, it isn't necessary for you to constantly pay attention to what I'm saying. You can go to wherever you feel most comfortable, and you'll hear me at an unconscious level."

Hahn glanced over at me and mouthed, *Watch this.*

"Okay, now, I want you to rub your pants leg with your right arm."

He moved his right arm down and began to rub his right pant leg.

"As you continue feeling your clothing with your fingers, your fingers and even your hand will get lighter. It will grow lighter and lighter. I don't know which finger feels the lightest, but one of them will feel so light it will begin to float, then the others will follow, then your wrist will feel so light it will begin to float, then your whole hand."

Within a minute, his right hand was floating out beside him, his arm dangling down as if an invisible cord was holding up his hand.

"Now you're going to lose all feeling in your floating hand. Do you feel it going numb? From your fingertips to your wrist, you have no feeling in your right hand."

She then took out a small needle and began to poke it into the tips of his fingers, tiny droplets of blood oozing out onto the skin and point of the needle as she did, but he showed no response whatsoever.

When I left Hahn's office, I found the nearest phone and called Hank Sproul back about the autopsy.

"It's John Jordan. Got a quick question for you."

"Okay."

"The pinpricks you mentioned, could they've been from testing the feeling in his hand?"

"Whatta you mean?" His voice rising, interested. "I guess that's possible. There nothing to suggest it's not. What in the world made you think of that?"

"Hypnotism," I said. "That's how hypnotists check to see if their patient is fully inducted."

Chapter Thirty-four

Walking back to my office, I ran into Emile Rollins.

"I just came from the chapel," he said. "I was hoping to talk to you."

He turned and fell into step with me.

"Is somebody tryin' to kill me—I mean the Kings?"

"I'm not sure."

"I feel like I'm in danger—more so than usual—and I's wondering if it's paranoia or . . ."

A school bell rang, and inmates poured out of the classrooms to our right the same way they must have when they were children. Many of them still were. Big, spoiled, obnoxious kids, unwilling or unable to grow up.

Several inmates passing by us were making fun of what they would be served that evening in the chow hall, and I was amazed again at their ingratitude and sense of entitlement.

He shook his head. "This place, man . . . Life is cheap. It's fuckin' bleak. Where's God?"

I shrugged. "Obscured by the bleakness maybe? I'm meant to be God's representative. But as usual . . . falling down on my job."

"No. I didn't mean . . . I just meant . . ."

"If God is love, works through love, then the

bleakness you're talking about is an absence of love."

Emile Rollins walked like a robot, his movements stiff and awkward, self-conscious—as if someone were watching him and it made him nervous or his joints didn't bend as far as they should.

"I wasn't really asking," he said. "It was just sort of rhetorical. I didn't want to be preached at."

Although Emile worked on an outside community work squad, his uniform was neatly pressed and spotless, and showed no sign of fading or wear, and I wondered if Brent Allen was taking care of his fellow Suicide King.

"You see Dr. Baldwin?" I asked.

"That relevant to my safety?"

I nodded.

"Yeah. She's good. Helped me more than anyone I've ever known."

"She use hypnotherapy on you?"

"Yeah," he nodded. "I don't know what it does, but it works. Works better than anything I've ever tried."

"You remember what you worked on when you come out?"

"No. I think that's the point."

"Anyone else ever hypnotize you?"

He shrugged. "She's taught a lot of us how to do it."

When we reached my office, my phone was ringing. I unlocked the door and rushed in to pick it up. Emile Rollins followed.

"Chaplain Jordan," I said into the receiver.

I hadn't been in my office much lately. The air was still and stale, the large plants in need of water. A fine patina of dust covered their leaves, my books, frames, and the pile of papers on my desktop. My chapel orderlies could only come in and clean when I was here to supervise them.

"Yes, Chaplain, this is Margaret Allen. An inmate incarcerated there, Brent Allen, is my son."

"Yes ma'am."

"His grandfather, Charles Allen, has been put in the hospital and I'd like for him to be able to call and talk to him. They don't expect him to make it through the night. It'd mean so much to him. My husband's dead and Brent is the only grandchild, the only family my father-in-law has."

"Yes, ma'am, I'm sorry to hear that," I said. "Let me get some information from you and I'll call Brent in and let him call the hospital as soon as possible."

"Thank you."

She gave me the information and we hung up.

"Brent's granddaddy?" Rollins said when I hung up the phone.

I didn't answer him.

"Well," he added, "guess I'll go so you can deal with that."

When I told Brent his grandfather was in the hospital, he nodded as if he'd been expecting the news, then just sat there, uninterested, inattentive.

"You okay?" I asked.

He nodded. "I've been expecting it, you know? I'm just glad it wasn't my mom. He's lived a long, prosperous life. He's had it good and easy."

"Would you like to call the hospital? I can get him on the line in here and you can talk to him in private."

"My mom still there?"

"I would think."

"Sure, let's do it."

His blank stare moved about my office as I punched in the number to the hospital. Nothing seemed to interest him. Not the plants, not the beautiful day beyond the window, not the colorful religious iconography. Nothing.

"Mom," he said into the phone when I handed it to him. "How are you? Yeah. Yeah. I'm good. No, really. I am. Mom, I'm not going to . . . I'm not even sad. I promise. I've got more reasons to live now than ever before."

He paused a moment.

"I really don't want to. He's not asleep or in a coma or something?"

He rolled his eyes while he listened.

"I wouldn't know what to say. No. Okay. I will. But listen, I need you to send me some money. My account's about empty. You know I need my canteen. It's all I've got. It's the only way I can survive in here. Understand? There'll be plenty now. Don't hold back."

He waited, making an unpleasant expression as he did.

Rarely did I grant an inmate a crisis phone call that he didn't ask his distraught family to send money. No matter how severe the crisis, how difficult the circumstance, far too often it seemed their primary purpose for calling.

It seemed Brent, like many of the men in here, was detached and dissociated from any emotional connections in his life.

"Grandpa . . . How are you?"

His voice was soft and filled with a concern his facial expressions and body language didn't confirm.

"Ah, you'll be fine," he said. "You'll see. You're a tough old bastard. You'll show them. Well . . . okay, then. Take care. Huh? Oh . . . yeah, me too."

He waited for another moment.

"Okay, Mom. Okay. Don't forget to send me some. Do it tonight. What? No. I need it now. Okay. Don't forget. You too. Bye."

Chapter Thirty-five

After Brent left, I walked to the kitchen in the back of the chapel for a cup of coffee. As I was about to walk back to my office, I heard what sounded like muffled screams coming from the inmate bathroom.

I dropped my cup on the counter and ran out of the kitchen, across the hallway, and into the bathroom.

Inside, I found Lance Phillips hanging from a thin rope that was tied to the top of the frame of the metal stall. His hands were bound at the wrists and he was struggling against the noose to no avail.

As I rushed over to help him, I detected movement to my right, and turned just in time to see a huge inmate wearing a white hood made from a pillowcase with eyeholes in it coming at me with a brass candle holder from the altar in the chapel.

He swung it down on me, but I ducked under it, threw my arms up and blocked it somehow.

The pain in my right arm hurt all the way down to the bone.

Lance shrieked and I turned toward him. He was losing consciousness. When I moved toward him, the big guy dropped the candle holder and dashed out of the restroom.

I ran over and grabbed Lance's legs and lifted him up. I held him that way for a minute as he gasped and coughed, trying to breathe.

I looked up at him. "You okay?"

He nodded.

I lifted him a little higher and he raised his arms and worked the noose from around his neck. I then eased him to the cold tile floor, amazed again at how easy it was to lift him. He looked anorexic, and he was lighter than he looked.

"If you're okay I wanna try to catch him before he leaves the chapel."

"Go ahead. I'm good."

I dashed out the door, back through the fellowship hall, and into the chapel. Lance was right behind me, and when I stopped abruptly he slammed into me.

We had run right into a small group of inmates, all of whom were wearing the pillowcase hoods to cover their faces.

They quickly surrounded us, putting us in the center of the circle they formed. They were all breathing heavily, their labored breaths coming fast and smelling bad.

"Chaplain, walk away now and you live."

They were all holding various weapons in their hands, from blunt objects found in the chapel to compound shivs and shanks.

I said, "I'll make you all the same offer."

They laughed at that . . .Until they saw Mr. Smith leading Merrill into the chapel.

Their laughter didn't fade, but stopped suddenly, as if it had been turned off.

They froze as he walked over toward us.

"It's just attempted assault," one of them said, easing

his shank toward the floor. "That's nothing. We cool."

Just before his shank touched the floor, he flicked his wrist, the shank straightening, and he lunged at me. Coming in low, he was falling forward more than rushing.

I brought my knee up and it connected, bone to cartilage, blood bursting from his broken nose. His neck snapped back and he fell to the floor, the shank falling quietly on the carpet as he did.

The others began to slowly place their weapons on the floor.

"We cool," another one said.

"We've heard that before," Merrill said. "Get your asses on the ground."

In another moment, all four inmates were on the ground.

"Those men were contract killers," I said. "It wasn't personal. They were doing it for someone else."

"That's what I figured," Lance said.

He shook his head slowly, tears welling up in his clear blue eyes.

We were in the infirmary where Dr. Alvarez had just finished examining him. He was reclined on the bed closest to the door, and I was standing next to him. We were the only two people in the infirmary.

"They have a king of hearts with them?" he asked.

"They had already put it in your pocket."

He nodded.

We were quiet a moment.

"Will they talk?" he asked.

I shook my head. "Don't think so. The charges are nothing compared to what they already have. If they're being paid as well as they say . . . they've got no reason to tell us anything."

"I get out soon. Got a great girlfriend. Big plans. I'm not safe. Could you have me transferred?"

I shook my head. "Don't have the authority. I can talk to Classification about it."

The tile floor beneath my feet gleamed with a shine to rival any hospital in the state, the result of excessive mopping, stripping, and waxing by inmate orderlies with not enough to do. The windows were as clear and as spotless as if they had not been there at all, but beyond them, the double chain-link fence and razor wire reminded us that no matter how clean it was, this was still a prison infirmary.

He nodded. "I'd appreciate it."

Through the square glass panes of the interior wall, I could see Dr. Alvarez walking down the hallway toward the medical conference room. He was walking slowly and seemed to be trying to overhear what we were saying.

"Guy gives me the creeps," Lance said. "If people knew the stuff he does down here. We're like his own little private collection of guinea pigs."

"He have a connection to the Suicide Kings?"

He shrugged. "We've all spent time down here."

Jamie Lee emerged from the back of the hallway, returning from a cigarette break. She smiled and waved as she walked by the open door, the smell of smoke and perfume swirling around her.

"What about Dr. Baldwin?"

"We've all been in her suicide prevention support group. We've all seen her individually. And we've all been in her hypnotherapy groups too."

"Tell me about the hypnotherapy."

"What's there to tell?" he said, rubbing the bandage on his neck absently. "She thinks it's the key to unlocking repressed traumas. She does a lot of regression therapy. You know, taking you back to certain critical events of childhood. She's good. She gets a lot of practice around here."

In front of me, the rows of toilets, sinks, and showers were dark and empty like the SOS cells across the way, but the officers' station behind us was lit and occupied by an officer, who with the push of one button could hear everything we were saying.

"Why all the interest in hypnotherapy, Chaplain?" Baldwin asked.

I turned to see her standing in the doorway.

"Find it fascinating."

"I believe in it," she said. "I really do, but never as a shortcut. I never use it when more traditional forms of treatment'll work just as well. Even if they take much longer. I care enough about my patients to invest the time. Right Lance?"

"Yes, ma'am," he said. "Absolutely."

"Can it be used to influence a patient to do something against his will?" I asked.

She was shaking her head before I finished.

"There's certainly some controversy and disagreement about that. But I for one firmly believe that even the strongest suggestion won't be taken if it's against the person's will."

"Haven't people in regression therapy falsely accused a parent or guardian of molesting them when they were children because a therapist planted the thought in their minds?"

"I am, of course, aware of such claims, but I haven't seen anything that's convinced me of it. I rather believe that the patients just backed down because of the social stigma and family pressure."

"But victims are in a very vulnerable and highly suggestible state when they're under hypnosis, right?"

"Patients," she said.

"Sorry?"

"You said *victims*. You meant *patients*. It's true, the inducted person is much more suggestible, but not to do things against his will."

"What if it's something that they don't have a strong will about either way," I said. "Is it possible to—"

"I don't believe so, but come by some time and I'll see what I can get you to do, okay?"

Chapter Thirty-six

"**R**ollins and Allen were in the chapel just before the latest attack on Lance," I said.

Merrill nodded.

"What if they're working together?" Anna asked.

I nodded. "Don't seem like the type that would, which might make it genius."

We were sitting in a booth in the back at Rudy's like we had so many times before, but this time Anna and I were together, had arrived together, would leave together, would go home together, would wake up together.

Wash. Rinse. Repeat. Ad infinitum.

"You ever talk to Donnie?" Merrill asked.

"Foster?" I shook my head.

"His name keep coming up."

"It does. I should have by now. I've tried a few times, but I've missed him. Just been following where the case leads, but, you're right, I need to—"

"I's just asking. Wasn't saying you should."

"His name keeps coming up 'cause he's a criminal," Anna said. "Also why he's avoiding you. If he's not involved in this, he's dirty on something."

She was right. He was one of the ones who shouldn't be allowed to go home at night.

Carla walked up with our food.

"Warden and inspector were in here talking about the case earlier," she said. "I eavesdropped on them. Overheard a lot."

"You did?"

"I'm so freakin' Veronica Mars."

"Yes you are," I said.

"Who?" Merrill asked.

She told him.

He shrugged indifferently.

Carla sat down beside him after placing our food on the table. All three of us were having a full breakfast of bacon, eggs, hash browns, grits, and pecan waffles. Anna was also having buttered biscuits and gravy, because the baby liked them.

"Love eatin' breakfast at night," Merrill said.

"Me too," Anna said.

"Me three," I said.

Carla looked at me. "You like everything better at night."

I smiled. "Want some?"

A look of horror appeared on her face. "You kidding? I don't eat the shit they serve here."

A trucker in Wrangler jeans, cowboy boots, and a flannel shirt sat at the far end of the counter, finishing up an omelet and his fourth cup of coffee. Draped over the bar chair beside him was a two-tone brown down vest.

"There's nothing wrong with it," she added. "I just eat, breathe, and sleep it every night. After a while you get sick of anything."

"Why I didn't become a gynecologist," Merrill said. "Sheeit, wife meet you at the door naked when come home from a long day at the office and you say, 'If I see one more . . .'"

We all laughed.

"So, what'd you accidentally overhear?" I asked.

She turned in the seat so she was facing me.

"Lawson believes it was a suicide. He's working real hard to convince Matson."

We ate while she talked. Carla made the best breakfast in Florida. Maybe in the South. Maybe in the world. When she finished talking, I had to wait a moment to respond because of all the good food in my mouth.

"Warden's not convinced?" I asked.

She shrugged and scrunched her face together to think about it. "I don't think so, but it's hard to tell much of anything with him."

Merrill smiled.

A bell dinged and Carla stood, bounced back behind the counter, and returned a moment later with a saucer piled high with toast, the butter dripping down the side of the stack.

Merrill and I looked at Anna.

"The baby likes bread," she said.

"Did he mention the attempt on Phillips?" I asked.

She nodded.

"And their connection?"

"The card? Said some inmate was trying to fuck with his head."

"He say where they got the rope?" Merrill said.

She shook her head. "Sorry."

"You did great. You heard a lot."

"I tried. Kept bringing stuff to their table. They thought I was the best waitress ever."

I looked at Merrill. "And I already found out about the rope. It was traced to two pieces missing from the maintenance department. Inmate probably snuck it in and sold it to them."

The trucker finished his coffee, wiped his mouth with a wadded up napkin, stood, put on his vest, zipped it up though it was a warm night, and walked out of the restaurant, waving to Carla as he did.

The four of us were now alone in the diner.

We were quiet a few minutes finishing our food. With strips of toast, Merrill wiped up the remaining grits and egg yolks and ate them. Just as we were finishing, Carla served us fresh, hot coffee and we drank it black, and it was good.

After a while, Carla said, "Could someone be trying to kill Phillips for a reason other than money?"

I nodded. "Could be anything."

"Yeah," Merrill said. "Reasons to kill a fool numerous as fools theyselves."

"And that," Anna added, smiling her radiant smile, "is the voice of experience."

Chapter Thirty-seven

That night Anna and I attended a political debate at the Pottersville Community Center.

Because of what happened at Potter Farm and the rumors about what happened, the place was packed with townspeople and reporters and news organizations.

Each candidate gave brief statements before the debate began.

Hugh Glenn worked what had happened at Potter Farm into his and questioned how something like that could happen right under the current sheriff's nose.

Dad's was brief and included assurances that he would be making an arrest in that case soon.

Ralph Long rambled on mostly about nothin', but in every single word he uttered he was begging to be liked, his neediness and desire to please so palpable it caused an uneasiness and awkwardness to permeate the room.

After bragging about his wisdom, integrity, and impartiality, Judge Richard Cox shared his certainty that the incident at Potter Farm was meant to bring embarrassment and shame to the Republican Party of Potter County in general and him in particular and was perpetrated by radical homosexuals as part of the gay agenda.

I looked across the room at Richie, who was sitting

next to his sister, Diane. He shook his head and rolled his
eyes, while next to him Diane's face flushed crimson.

Don Stockton was smug and cocky and the only
candidate certain of his reelection.

"I'm not an educated man," Stockton said, "so I'll
have to defer to the good judge's opinion on such matters,
but in my experience, nine times out of ten the motive
for everything comes down to money. It's what makes the
world go round. It's what everybody wants and nobody has
enough of. So whether it's a gay agenda or a straight agenda
. . . it's gonna include a green agenda. Promise you that."

After the formal debate had concluded and the
moderator opened it up to questions from the audience,
every single question but one was about what had
happened at Potter Farm and the body of the blonde
victim murdered there.

The one question not related to Potter Farm was still
directed at Dad.

It was asked by Chris Taunton, Anna's soon-to-be,
but not soon enough, ex.

"Sheriff, is it true that your son, a supposed minister
of the Gospel, is shackin' with another man's pregnant
wife?" he said. "And if so, how do you expect voters to
reelect a man who would raise such an immoral sack of shit
hypocrite?"

I took Anna's hand, as the majority of those in
attendance turned to glance at us.

"I'm so sorry," she whispered.

"Why? You didn't do anything."

"I married the motherfucker."

"We all do foolish things in our youth," I said.

"What I did was far worse."

"What's that?"

"Left here without you."

"That's true," she said. "This is all your fault."

At the conclusion of the event, my instinct was to duck out the nearest door, but Anna convinced me to stay and face our accusers with our scarlet *A*s displayed proudly.

When we finally reached the friendly face of Richie Cox, I breathed a little easier.

"Dir," he said to his sister, "you remember my friend the supposed minister of the Gospel shackin' with another man's pregnant wife immoral sack of shit hypocrite, don't you?"

"He looks familiar," Diane said, "but . . . the name's not ringing any bells."

Richie extended his hand to Anna. "Hi I'm Richie Cox. I'm part of the gay agenda trying to destroy the world and keep my dad from being reelected."

"Nice to meet you," she said. "Let me know any way I can help you with that."

"This is his sister, Dirty Diana," I said. "The one who said you were lucky to be with me."

They shook hands.

I looked at Diane. "Sure you don't want to amend your opinion on the subject?"

She shook her head. "You guys are so lucky to have each other."

"Yes we are," Anna said.

"This was fun," Richie said.

"Wasn't it?" Anna said. "And to think I almost didn't come."

"I love my dad," Diane said. "And I think he's a pretty good judge, but . . . I don't know . . . maybe it wouldn't be the worst thing in the world if none of them got reelected."

Richie shook his head. "I'm gonna be honest. I'm not ready for the lifestyle change. The way the economy is . . . If the judge didn't supplement my income . . . yours too . . . No, my gay agenda is to keep his homophobic ass in office."

Diane looked over my shoulder, her eyes widening as she did.

I turned to see Hugh Glenn approaching from one direction and Chris Taunton from another.

Hugh reached us first.

"You need to reason with your dad," he said to me. "He's making some outlandish accusations."

"Such as?"

"Such as me having somethin' to do with that girl's death in order to win the election."

"Who was the first person to bring it up tonight?" I said. "In an attempt to win the election."

"Think about what you're sayin'," he said. "Talk some sense into your dad."

"It's the father that needs to talk some sense into the son," Chris said as he reached us.

I turned toward him, stepping in front of Anna.

"You don't have to protect her from me," he said.

I didn't respond.

"That's my wife."

"I'm not *your* anything," she said, coming around to stand beside me. "And if you don't stop acting so petulant and stop stalking me, I'm gonna make a few public statements of my own. Understand? I've guarded your dignity so far, kept your secrets, but you ever pull another juvenile stunt like that again and I'm gonna shine a very bright light on you. Now walk away without another word."

He thought about it without saying anything. She had gotten through to him.

"Walk away, Chris," she said.

And in another moment he did.

Chapter Thirty-eight

My mom died the next day.

I couldn't be sure, but there was no evidence she took her own life. And even if I could know for sure she didn't, it wouldn't mitigate the guilt and regret I felt.

I had gotten so wrapped up in my relationship with Anna and what was going on inside the prison with the Suicide Kings and outside with the missing blonde murder victim, that I had neglected her during her final days.

Sometimes it seemed as though I was surrounded on all sides by death. Daily, I received reminders that long life is an illusion, that our existence, regardless of the length, was but a vapor, quickly floating up to vanish into nothingness. Here then gone.

As I drove over to meet Dad and Jake at her house, I recalled the one time in the last few days I had made it by to see her . . .

It hadn't been late, but Mom was sleeping, waking occasionally for brief exchanges before drifting off again.

I sat by her bed thinking about death and dying, about how very brief our time here was, how we lost everything eventually, inevitably, and what a tragedy that was.

Her eyes fluttered open. "Sorry I can't wake up."

"Don't be."

"I'm just so tired today."

"Just rest," I said. "I'm gonna sit here a while. I'll slip out later."

She dozed off again, her breathing labored, her rest fitful, her body constantly twitching and jerking.

I had been watching Mom die for quite a while now. Now that she had, it wasn't unexpected, I wasn't shocked or caught off guard, but I also wasn't prepared for it. There was nothing I could've done to be, nothing I knew to do anyway.

"I'm not going to," Mom had said.

Her eyes had been closed and at first I thought she was talking in her sleep.

"If you're worried about . . ."

She opened her eyes and looked over at me, straining to keep her heavy lids from falling shut.

"Ma'am?"

"I'm gonna let things take their natural course . . . I'm not gonna . . . put an end to this myself."

I nodded and smiled and took her hand in mine.

"Thank you, John," she said. "For everything. For all you've done. For . . . everything."

Those had been the last words I would ever hear her say.

Over the next three days of dealing with Mom's death and preparing to officiate her funeral, I only entered the institution twice. Once to meet with Brent Allen. The other to meet with the warden and the chaplain supervisor about my immorality.

"My granddad?" Brent Allen asked when he walked

into my office.

I nodded. "I'm very sorry."

I had been called back in to the institution to notify him that his grandfather had died. He had been escorted to my office by an officer, who remained in the hallway. The officer accompanied him not only because it was dark and the yard was closed, but in case he became crazed or violent. It was standard operating procedure. Inmates receiving death notifications were accompanied by officers whether the yard was open or not. But I didn't expect any behavioral problems from Brent.

"That was fast," he said, sinking down into one of the chairs across from my desk.

I nodded.

Except for the officer in the hallway, we were alone in the chapel—alone in the upper compound except for Medical. Like the compound, the chapel was dark and quiet, the only lights on were in the hallway and my office, the only sounds, the ones we were making—and we weren't making any at the moment.

"How are you?" I asked.

He was looking down, seemingly deep in thought, eyes narrowed, lips pursed, hand absently rubbing the back of his head.

He lifted his head and looked at me. "Huh?"

"How are you?"

"I'm okay. Been expecting it—not this fast, but . . . I don't know . . . it's . . . to lose someone like him while I'm in here. Makes the rethink all my bullshit about suicide and death."

"Really?"

It seemed sudden, unearned if not exactly insincere, but maybe he really had been shocked into reconsideration.

"It's all so . . . out of our control, you know? How

can I be so cavalier about my potential death when all he
wanted to do was live a little longer and there was nothing
he could do . . . Anyway, gives me something to think
about."

With this last statement, his demeanor changed with
his posture. He sat up and perked up, even smiling at me.
"Thanks," he said.

"You sure you're okay?"

He nodded.

"Not angry? Frustrated? Don't feel the desire to hurt
yourself or someone else?"

He smiled. "I'm fine. I really am. I'm . . . It's just that
. . . I didn't expect to feel anything at all . . . but—and it's
not sadness. It's just . . . I don't know . . . got me thinking."

"You wanna call your mom?"

"Not now. I will later. From the dorm is fine."

"I'll make sure the dorm officers know about your
situation. They'll turn on the phones for you when you get
ready. If you need me, just let them know."

"Sounds good. Thanks again."

He stood, seemingly a different man than when he
sat.

He shook his head. "It just happened so much faster
than I thought it would. I feel like someone just sucker
punched me."

I knew how he felt.

"Chaplain Jordan, I'm gonna be honest with you,"
Chaplain Cunningham said. "I'm very disappointed in your
behavior."

He was an overweight, middle-aged white man with
wavy brown hair and glasses. A Southern Baptist literalist,
Fundamentalist, his narrow worldview and rigid belief

system made my religion unrecognizable to him.

We were in Matson's office. Just the three of us—me, Matson, and Cunningham. The door was closed.

"You've always been on the fringes," Cunningham continued. "Haven't ever really fit in with the rest of us."

There were about a hundred prison chaplains in the state and apparently I had never really fit in with them.

"I've tolerated a certain amount of unorthodox behavior out of you because . . . well, you're liked and respected by your coworkers and the inmates you serve and . . . I guess I kept thinkin' you'd find the way. But we're here to help lost men find their way, not to give you time to find yours. How can the blind lead the blind?"

"What he's sayin', Chaplain," Matson said, "you've been given plenty of rope but rather than climb up it you've hung yourself with it."

I nodded. I knew this day would come. In truth, I had lasted longer than I expected.

He was right. I didn't fit in with him, his agenda, or the other chaplains. And I never would.

"I'm just afraid you've lost your moral authority," Cunningham said. "Living with another man's pregnant wife. It's a double sin."

I didn't say anything. Just listened.

"Now brother, hear me out on this," he said. "I've prayed about it and I believe God wants you to step down, to resign your position. Chaplain Singer's a good man. He can step in when he returns and see to the spiritual needs of the compound. The institution will be in good hands. Whatta you say? Will you do the right thing? From what I understand you'd be happier being some sort of police officer anyway."

Suddenly I was his brother and he was asking me not telling me to go.

"You're asking me to quit?" I said.

"To find somethin' that's a better fit for you. You must feel that you don't fit here."

But must I feel I don't fit anywhere?

"You're not firing me? You're asking me to . . . find a better fit?" I asked, hearing the incredulity in my own voice.

I had found somewhere I fit, hadn't I? I fit with Anna. We fit as if formed for one another, as if we always had, as if what Rumi had written was particularly and uniquely true of us. Lovers don't finally meet somewhere. They're in each other all along.

"We're giving you the opportunity to resign instead of firing you," Matson said. "Why not do yourself a favor and leave with some dignity? If you will . . . if you'll go quietly today, no fuss, no muss, I'll give you a glowing letter of reference."

"If I don't quit, when will you fire me exactly?"

"Don't let it come to that," Cunningham said. "Do the right thing."

"Do you have any idea how many times I've thought about quitting?" I said. "Do you have any idea how much easier my life would be if I did? You're right, I don't fit in with you and the warden and the other chaplains, and you all remind me of just how much every chance you get. But I do a lot of good here. I know I do. I see the fruit of it in the inmates and the staff in the trenches, in the grit and grind of everyday life here—somethin' you'll never see from your office in Tallahassee. You don't like me. I get it. You don't approve of me or my theology or my lifestyle. Fine. You don't have to. But I'm not quitting. I'm not going anywhere until you finally force me to, which if you were able you would've already done instead of asking me to resign. If I'm wrong about that then fire me on the spot because you won't get my resignation willingly—if only because you want it so bad and part of me wants nothing more than to give it to you."

"Don't think we can't fire you," Matson said. "This is my prison. I can—"

"Chaplain Jordan," Cunningham said. "Our attorneys are looking into it. Eventually they'll find a way for us to . . . but why not save us all the hassle and go quietly?"

"See previous answer," I said. "Now, if you have nothing more to say to me, I've got to go bury my mother."

Neither of them said anything and I walked out.

Chapter Thirty-nine

I really didn't remember much of what I said at Mom's funeral.

I remembered how sad the whole thing was, how pathetic and poorly attended, how awkward Nancy and Jake looked on either side of Dad, how bad Mom looked lying in the coffin, how the quiet church creaked, how everyone looked at me as I attempted to honor this woman I had had such a complicated relationship with, how I had mostly just looked at Anna.

I remembered confessing to the small crowd how lost and alone I felt, how numb, how inept I felt at doing something I had done so many times before.

I remarked on how surprised I was by how affected I was by the loss of her, how even given the grace of so much time to prepare, I wasn't prepared at all. Not really.

I shared how I felt vulnerable in a way I never had before. Abandoned. Exposed. Like the last of the little barrier island between me and the vast senseless sea, between me and death, had finally finished its erosion and washed away forever, that between me and the grave gone.

I read the obituary I had written. And then the eulogy.

I tried to tell them, her friends and family, what she was like when she was controlling her addiction, and a little, for integrity and honesty's sake, what she was like when it was controlling her.

I told them of the fun times and firm foundation she provided for me when I was young—something that had given me the strength to deal with the later ways her abuse of alcohol ravaged our lives.

I re-created the adventures she had taken me on— our day trips to Wakulla Springs and the Junior Museum, the capitol and the beach, the summer nights at Miracle Strip and the skating rink—the elaborate Christmases, the extravagant birthdays, the ordinary days at home building a tree fort outside or a sheet and blanket tent inside, making homemade ice cream and peanut butter and jelly sandwiches and watching Saturday morning cartoons.

She had been a good mom when it mattered most, when we were young and forming, and a difficult and challenging mother when we were adults, something that, through grace, had been changing for some time now.

I did pretty well, held it together until Merrill's mom, the woman who would always be Mama Monroe to me, came up to me after the graveside service and wrapped me up in her massive arms.

Merrill was there with her, beside her, but didn't say anything. He had already said all he needed to say and I needed to hear, but what meant the most was what went without saying, what he didn't have to verbalize because of the lifetime of his extraordinary friendship.

"I'm your mama now, boy, understand?" Mama said.

I began to cry.

"You sort of already were," I said when I could.

"No sorta now, shuga," she said. "I'm your mama."

Merrill nodded.

"Mama hear you need somethin' a mama can do and you didn't call her, Mama gonna be mighty unhappy with you. Understand?"

"Yes, ma'am. Thank you."

"You really captured her," Nancy said. "You were truthful and kind—something I'd've said couldn't have been done where she was concerned."

I had found her having a cigarette in the shadow of an oak tree cast in the back corner of the cemetery.

She had been out of my life so long, it was like I didn't have a sister, and the too-thin, stylishly dressed New Yorker in front of me was as much stranger as anything else.

"I'm glad you came," I said.

"Started not to. You can't imagine how close I came to not coming."

Most everyone who had attended the internment were still milling about Mom's awning-covered graveside, visiting, comforting, reminiscing.

"How are you?" I asked.

"Don't try to counsel me, John," she said.

"I'm not."

"I was doing okay," she said. "Things are goin' well for me. Having to come back here . . . for this . . . is going to regress me some, but . . ."

She held her cigarette up slightly and considered it. "Haven't had one of these in . . . a very long time. Had to bum it from creepy old Hugh Glenn. Can you believe he's here?"

All of them were—all those in office, all those running for office, all the suspects from the killing at Potter Farm.

"Dad would be there if Imogene died."

"He would, wouldn't he?" she said, shaking her head. "Haven't missed any of the polite political bullshit."

"Didn't think you had missed anything."

"I've missed you, little brother," she said. "That's a fact. More now that I've seen you. Can't believe you and Anna are finally together. That only took fuckin' forever."

"And you and love?" I asked.

"There's someone," she said. "For a while now. Actually met in AA."

I nodded.

"You're trying not to act surprised," she said. "Didn't know I was a friend of Bill W.'s, did you?"

"I'm not surprised," I said. "I'm happy for you."

"He's good for me and to me."

"I'm so glad to hear that," I said. "So glad."

"Though I'm having second thoughts now," she said. "Since I arrived and found you with my best friend, thought it only fair if I get with yours."

I laughed out loud at the thought of Nancy and Merrill.

"You're right," she said. "I'm probably too much woman for him."

We were quiet a moment.

"She lasted longer than I thought she would," she said. "Wonder how much longer we have Dad for? Not that her death will have any impact on him . . . but he's gettin' up there."

"He may not be the next family member to go," I said.

"Did I tell you I had a meeting in the World Trade Center the morning of nine-eleven?"

I shook my head.

She hadn't told me anything in a very, very long time.

"I should be dead. Really just a comedy of errors that I'm not."

"I'm so glad you're still here," I said. "And here. How long you staying?"

"Fly out this afternoon," she said.

"**Y**ou're an amazing man," Anna said.

It was late. We were finally alone for the first time since we had woken up together the morning before.

We were lying in our bed in the dark, her head on my chest, her thick, beautiful brown hair draped over me.

"I don't know anyone who could've done what you did," she said. "You were so graceful and elegant, yet honest and elegiac."

I was exhausted, emotionally spent, spiritually depleted. Her kind, overly complimentary words were a soothing salve for my soul, her warm bare skin on mine, healing and whole-making.

"Thank you," I said. "You can't know what that means to me."

"I'm showing great restraint in what I'm saying," she said. "Holding back. Choosing every word carefully. Could easily add a hundred for each."

"So sweet."

"I'm not being sweet. I'm in awe of you. More now than ever. There's no way what you did could've been easy or effortless, but that's the way you made it look."

"You know what I kept thinking today? It was no different than any other day these days. I kept thinking, I get to go home with Anna. I'm the lucky man who gets to lie next to her tonight."

"Every night," she said. "I kept thinkin' the same thing. That amazing man, saying such beautiful and insightful things, that man who I respect and admire more than any other I've ever known, is mine. I get to go home with him tonight. Wake with him tomorrow."

She may have said more, but those were the last words I heard before I succumbed to the heavy-handed demands of the sandman.

Good night, moon. Good night, Mom. Good night, sweet, beautiful Anna. Good night, world for a while.

Chapter Forty

I was headed to a crime scene when Hahn called.

"I pulled Bailey's file from Personnel," she said.

"What?" I asked in shock. "I really wish you hadn't done that."

"Not when you hear what I found out."

I was on the mostly desolate highway that connected Pottersville and Panama City, the early morning light filtering down through the slash pines, shining through the rows onto the road in shafts of bright yellow and orange.

"She's not licensed by the state."

"*What?*" I said.

Up ahead on my right I could see an enormous clear-cut field where just days before there had been a thirty-year-old flatlands pinewood forest.

It looked as if a massive super storm had blown through and leveled the land, leaving a gaping swath of baldness where once had been life and beauty. The devastation of deforestation.

Skidders were crawling through the fallen forest, twisting and turning like mechanical animals as they pinched and pulled the felled trees toward waiting log trucks.

Pulling off the highway, I turned down a dirt road,

where on each side slash pines were being harvested.

"She was appointed with the provision she would obtain her license within a year, which ends next month. Somebody had to want her to have this job very badly."

I thought about who that might be.

"And she doesn't have a legitimate degree. Her PhD is mail-order. Unaccredited. Which is why she's having trouble getting licensed. And she told me she could supervise me for the hours I need for licensure. Now I've got to start over."

"Better to know now," I said.

Very little was left standing for hundreds of acres—the occasional oak tree, a small stand of cypress trees rimming a small patch of wetland, a handful of homemade tree stands, and a small, one-room mobile home cut in half, the two pieces separated by a narrow debris field about ten feet long.

"She's had problems at her last two places of employment. Left in a hurry both times. She claims she's been the victim of sexual harassment, but has never so much as filed a complaint."

"Where'd she work?"

"Medical clinic in Pensacola. And get this. It's the same one Alvarez was fired from."

I pulled up not far from the last in a line of emergency vehicles and turned off the car.

"Thank you," I said. "That's very helpful, but please don't ever do anything like that again."

"Yes sir."

"The hypnotherapy demonstration you did for me—was that a pretty normal session?" I asked.

"I haven't done that many. But it's pretty standard from what I've experienced. He's easier to induct than most people. Why I chose him."

"Raising his arm, his hand going numb—what all can you get him to do?"

"Well, they're just suggestions. You can suggest anything, but his subconscious has to be willing to do it. Hypnosis puts him in a state of less resistance, but he can still resist anything that he normally would be uncomfortable with consciously. I only use it after several sessions of therapy, and then only to deal with what comes up during therapy. If he can't remember anything before he was eight . . . I'll regress him back and see what happened."

"His subconscious will remember?"

"Every detail. It's amazing. You've never heard detail like this. Our subconscious minds record everything. We take him back, let him remember it, relive it, then help him bring it up into the conscious so we can deal with it. But I do very little regression therapy. It takes enormous skill. You can do so much damage. Some patients remember things that they and the therapist aren't prepared for, and it devastates them to such an extent they never recover."

"So the patient remembers when they come out of it? I mean, what was said or remembered while they were under."

"Unless the therapist tells them not to."

"That's possible?"

"They're in a highly suggestible state. You can tell them not to remember and they won't."

"You could suggest that they do something, and tell them not to remember you suggesting it?"

"Yeah. Everyone's different. But you can get some people to do almost anything—as long as they aren't morally opposed to it. Some people believe with continuous suggestion you could get someone to even do something against their will, but I don't know. You might get them to do some things, but nothing like . . ."

"Kill?" I offered.

"Honestly, I don't know. I don't think you could most people, but there's a hell of a lot we don't know about the mind. Everybody's different. There's an exception to every rule. Plus, there's a whole hell of a lot of guys in here who aren't morally opposed to anything."

I clicked off the call and sat for a moment, breathing, thinking, enjoying the sun streaming in my windows.

Eventually, Jake walked up and I got out.

"Mornin'," he said.

"Morning," I said. "How are you?"

"Sad," he said. "You?"

"Same."

"Don't feel like myself," he said. "It's weird."

I nodded and we were silent a moment.

Finally he jerked his head back toward the crime scene and said, "Nothin' like a little violent death to force us to let life go on."

"Whatcha got?"

"Caucasian male. Early twenties. Shot in the head with a shogun. Looks self-inflicted but . . . ME is looking now. He was in that old trailer. It'd been dragged out here for hunters to use. Loggers didn't even know it was there until the skidder backed through it. Guy's naked. No clothes or shoes or identification anywhere in or around the trailer. He was just sitting in an old chair, the shotgun leaning against him."

I nodded and we started walking toward the trailer.

"Oh," Jake said, "I keep forgetting to tell you. Nobody seems to know anything about the cold-case card deck but Potter. He said they were already there from a previous game and we just pulled them out of the drawer when we needed them. Says there's more in the drawer."

I nodded. "Thanks."

"Is that something?"

"I thought it might be," I said, "but I don't think it is. Just a coincidence. Thanks for checking."

"Sure. I can look further if I need to."

As we neared the crime scene, I could see that everything was pretty much as Jake had described except for one crucial thing. The guy had not shot himself. He hadn't even been alive when it happened.

I looked closer.

The small, nude young man, a boy really, his decaying corpse on display for everyone to gawk at, was pale and pathetic, his hairless body narrow and soft.

He was splayed out in an old, large cloth chair, his head flopped back on the top, his arms dangling down beside him, his legs extending out on the partial floor of the torn-asunder trailer.

Dad walked over to us.

"How are you, son?"

"Okay," I said. "You?"

"You did a damn fine job on your mom's funeral," he said. "I was very proud of you."

I nodded the thanks I was unable to utter at the moment.

He turned back to look at the ME examining the body.

"Sure was hoping this was going to be a hunting accident or even a suicide," he said.

"It's not?" Jake said.

I shook my head.

"See how there's no blood or bruising around the gunshot wound," I said. "He was already dead when it happened, and dead men don't bleed."

"That's exactly what the ME said," Dad added.

"But he's got some dried blood on him," Jake said. "And some bruising."

I nodded. "Happened before he was shot."

"A few more miles that way and this would've been in Bay County," Dad said.

"Yeah," Jake said.

"Doesn't look like it's going to be quick and easy," Dad added. "Could very well turn into another open unsolved by the time the election gets here."

I started to say something but my phone rang.

It was the prison.

I stepped a few feet away to take the call and was informed that Brent Allen had been found dead, hanging from his bunk in the exact same manner as Danny Jacobs.

Chapter Forty-one

Déjà vu.

The inmate hanging from the top bunk could've been Danny Jacobs. The body fell forward against the rope the same way, the head leaning over the noose at an unnatural angle. The dry, swollen tongue protruded the same way. The lifeless arms dangled like Danny's had.

But it wasn't Danny Jacobs.

The latest victim of an apparent suicide at Potter Correctional Institution was the Suicide King himself, Brent Allen.

The same type of small cord looked to have been used on or by Allen. He was in the exact same location and position where Jacobs had been found, a suicide king playing card sticking out of his waistband.

It was all so similar, but from the moment I walked up to the body, I knew this death was different.

The fixed lividity, which was wrong for the position of the body, and the marks made by the rope were inconsistent with the way his neck hung in the noose.

"Maybe we been watching the wrong convict," Merrill said.

He was standing near me, looking at the body.

I frowned and shook my head. "Maybe so."

"Maybe not," Officer Wilder said, edging over toward us. "He was sleeping in Phillips's bunk."

Derek Wilder, an evening shift officer who had no reason to be in here, had been listening in on our conversation since it started—something I found annoying until he stepped up with useful information.

I called Lance over from where the dorm officers had the inmates lined up preparing to relocate them to one of the empty T-cell dorm quads.

"Brent was in your bunk last night?"

Lance reached up and rubbed his neck. "I was so sore and stove up from what happened in the chapel, he traded bunks with me. I's having a hard time climbing up on the top bunk."

"Fucker really did want to die," Merrill said.

"He thought he was invincible, but honestly, we didn't even think about it. I mean, I wouldn't've been down here if I didn't think it was safe. No one thought anyone would try something here again. And we figured the dorm officers would be watching us—this back corner—a lot more closely now."

I turned and looked across the dorm at Donnie Foster.

"I just don't get you dumb bastards," Merrill said.

Lance shrugged. "I don't want to die. Never did. I'm not sure any of us did—but a few didn't seem to care much either way. Brent was one of 'em. None of this should've ever happened. It was just something to do, a way to pass the time."

I shook my head.

Merrill said, "Lawson and company gonna be here any minute. Anything else you need to—"

As if on cue, the door opened and Mark Lawson

walked in. Merrill and I began walking out. No reason to
have him kick us out when we could leave voluntarily. We
met him halfway between where we had been and the door.

"Chaplain," he said in a congenial voice. "Just the
man I was looking for. I've been told to eat some humble
pie and ask you to help us on this one."

I was so surprised I didn't know what to say. I was
also suspicious as hell.

"Come on," he said, beginning to move toward the
back of the dorm and the body awaiting him there. "Let's
take a look and see what we got."

Merrill and I both followed him.

I had guessed that Mark Lawson would be the kind
of man to make jokes at a crime scene, and when he began
I was disappointed I had been right about him.

"Don't understand why everybody's killing
themselves," he said. "We doing something wrong? They
not happy here?"

We didn't respond.

"So's this guy part of the suicide club?"

I nodded. "The Suicide Kings."

"I'm thinkin' we need to ship the rest of 'em off to a
psych camp. Keep 'em from killing themselves."

"He was murdered," I said.

"How can you be so sure?" Lawson said. "They
haven't even done an autopsy on him."

"Lividity doesn't match the position of the body."

He took a closer look at the body. "I'll be damned."

Brent's lividity was fixed. The entire front portion of
his body was bruised, and his feet, which were the lowest
points in his current position, weren't any darker than any
other part of him. The body had been moved after he was
murdered.

He had been lying facedown when he was killed.
After he was dead, he had been left that way for a while—
probably as the killer waited for the right time to string
him up—and it was long enough for the lividity to become
fixed. Later, when he was moved, tied up in the position
he was in now, the discoloration of his skin from the
facedown position he had been killed and left in didn't
change.

"Look at the marks on his neck," I said. "See how
the bruise is in a straight line like a ring?"

Lawson looked. "Yeah?"

"If he'd really been hung, it wouldn't be a circle, but
a V. The pressure of the rope where it's tied above the head
causes it to pull up. Looks like he was strangled facedown
on his bunk or on the floor, killed, left there for a while,
then hung from the bunk."

Walking over to Donnie Foster in the far corner of the
dorm, I said, "You've been avoiding me."

"Sure I ain't the only one."

"Oh really?"

"You jam people up."

"Actually, he help people out," Merrill said.

"Got nothin' I need help with," Foster said.

"Got anything you could get jammed up for?" I
asked.

"No. Haven't done anything. Haven't seen anything.
Don't know anything. Don't want any trouble. Won't say
anything else."

Merrill stepped toward him.

"You can't scare me or threaten me or coerce me

into telling you something I don't know. I ain't gonna make shit up. And I won't stand here and just keep saying the same thing over and over."

He then walked away and we let him.

Chapter Forty-two

Clarissa was crying.

The small apartment was sad and dingy and smelled of years of cheap food, cigarette and pot smoke, dogs, cats, birds, people, paint, perms, bleach, air freshener, carpet cleaner, and a thousand other things in layer upon layer of lives lived in a cramped, inexpensive place.

The apartment was right off Balboa in Panama City, just a couple of miles from the college.

Clarissa King lived here now and was adding a new layer of her own.

She was a short, round black girl in her early twenties, nearly as wide as she was tall.

I was here because she had filed a missing person's report recently of a young man I was pretty sure was the victim who had been found by the loggers in the hunting trailer.

His name was Andy Bearden. He was her roommate. And the more she told me about him, the more I became convinced it was him.

"But Andy didn't hunt," Clarissa said. "He wouldn't've been out there hunting. He could never shoot anything. Couldn't hurt a fly. One of the gentlest souls you'd ever want to meet."

I nodded.

"Do you really think it could be him?" she asked, dotting tears from the corners of her eyes with the tips of her fat fingers.

"That's what I'm tryin' to find out."

"But who would kill him? No one would kill him. He didn't have an enemy in the world."

"When was the last time you saw him?"

She thought about it. "Can't be sure exactly. Our schedules are so different and we stay so busy and I just got back from visiting my people in Louisiana. I've been gone a week and it was probably a few days before that. I'm just not sure."

"Tell me some more about him."

"He was the sweetest, kindest boy," she said. "Don't get me wrong, he'd fight like hell for the underdog, for what he believed in. He was sort of scrappy, but he couldn't do much. He was so little."

"He been scrappin' with anyone in particular lately?"

She shook her head. "I don't think so. But he was always taking up lost causes, helping the helpless and hopeless, sharing and giving what he had until he ran out. Perfect example—this is his apartment. He's just letting me stay here and pay what I can, which isn't a lot. We're in college together over at Gulf Coast. He's on scholarship, gets grants and shit. Me, not so much. He shares it all until it runs out."

"What's he studying?"

"Theater. We both are. It's how we met. He's such a great performer. So dramatic. So brave and committed. Was always blowing me away with the places he would go—so vulnerable, so brave."

"Are you two romantically involved?"

She laughed a little and shook her head. "I don't really go for white guys—especially if they weigh less than one of my legs—and he didn't go for girls of any color or size."

"And you can't think of anyone who'd want to hurt him?"

"No. No way."

"Nothing he was mixed up in that might have caused him to cross paths with dangerous people?"

"No. Absolutely not. He was a straightedge, a real clean kid, you know? Never got involved in anything illegal or even sketchy. Only thing he ever did that was the least bit edgy was gay pride stuff. Marches. Sit-ins. Protests. Marriage equality rallies. Stuff like that. But even then, he was so sweet about it, so gentle and kind—even to the ignorant assholes on the other side of the issue."

"Does he have a boyfriend?"

"He's single. Has been a long time. He's got friends. Lots of them. He sleeps with some of 'em sometimes, but it's more cool and casual than you can imagine."

"Where'd he work?"

"Full-time student. I mean, he did some performances. Shows, plays, musicals. Like that. Never makes more than beer money and he actually loses money when he does the drag shows at places like the Fiesta in town and Splash Bar on the beach. The costumes are so elaborate and expensive. Wait. I just thought of something."

"What's that?"

"He's got a thing for straight guys and . . . oh wow . . ."

"What is it?"

"Where'd you say he was killed? He used to meet a closeted country boy from Pottersville out in the woods between here and there. Called him Roughneck Redneck.

This was a while back. Hasn't mentioned him in forever . . . I thought he had stopped seeing him. Think he had. But what if he met him again?"

"Can you think of anything else about him? A name? Description? Anything?"

She thought about it. "It's been a while. He was married. Paranoid. Petrified of being found out. Ron. I think one time he said Ron the Roughneck Redneck . . . but I can't be sure. Got the feeling he was a pretty big guy. Or maybe he just had a big dick. I can't remember. I'm sorry."

"You've been very helpful," I said. "Thanks for taking the time to talk to me. If you think of anything else . . . please give me a call."

I gave her my number and a hug and left.

Walking back to my car, I called Richie Cox.

"Don't tell me we've got another political event," he said. "I honestly think I'd shoot myself in the face rather than face another one of those dreadful things."

"Calling on a different matter."

"Oh yeah? What's that?"

I told him.

"I'm completely out of the closet," he said. "I'm as gay as a Christmas pageant and everybody knows it. But I truly sympathize with those who can't come out—or don't feel like they can. It's a lot more guys than you think. Public figures. Married men. Preachers. Men who would lose their families and jobs and more if they ever dared to be truthful about who they really are."

"Wish we lived in a different world," I said.

"We're making it one," he said.

"Maybe."

"Thing is," he said, "guys living double lives, hiding so much of who they are, can be full of rage and self-hatred. That kind of compartmentalized duality . . .

Wouldn't surprise me if someone like that snapped. You know if they loathe themselves then they loathe who they're involved with even more."

"Can you think of anyone in our area who fits the description?" I asked. "Maybe or maybe not named Ron. Maybe a big guy."

"There's something . . ." he said. "I can't quite put my finger on it. No one's coming to mind, but I feel like some part of me knows something and I just can't remember it right now."

"Think of something else," I said. "Call me when it comes to you."

"Will do. And John."

"Yeah?"

"Thanks for caring about us fags."

I had reached my car and was about to get in when Clarissa yelled to me from her door.

She loped over toward me, the massive mounds of her belly and breasts bouncing about as she did.

"His brother."

"Yeah?"

"Sorry," she said, trying to catch her breath. "Wasn't gonna say anything 'cause I'm a little scared of him, but . . . his brother's a crackhead meth dealer. He was always in trouble—and always tryin' to get Andy to bail him out, help him out, give him money, let him crash here. I wonder if something his sketchy ass is involved in got Andy killed. If he got Andy killed, I'll kill him. Swear to God."

"Any idea where I can find him?"

"He works at some shady clinic. When he works at all. Just does it to steal pills. Why does someone like him get to live and a sweet boy like Andy get murdered? The fuck is wrong with this world?"

Chapter Forty-three

Merrill and I were on our way to Alverez's clinic when Lawson called.

"It's Inspector Lawson. They rushed the autopsy and we got a conference call goin'. Gonna patch you in."

"Why are you suddenly including me?" I asked.

"Want this job," he said. "Need your help. Warden treated me like shit one too many times. Hold on. Here we go."

The line clicked and beeped and we were joined by the pathologist.

"Go ahead, Doc," Lawson said.

Because it was a multi-line conference call, the connection was airy and very difficult to hear.

"The victim was dead before he was hung," the voice I didn't recognize said.

Everything was being made to look like something other than what it was. Murders staged to look like suicides. Same thing done to Andy Bearden and Danny Jacobs.

"Y'all were right about the lividity," he continued. "He died facedown and then stayed there for several hours before he was hung. The bruises on his neck indicates strangulation. We also found bruising at the base of the skull where the murderer exerted pressure. The vessels in the neck were occluded, the face and neck were congested and dark red. There were also some abrasions and contusions on the neck from the force required to kill him. It fractured the hyoid bone . . . thyroid cartilage. Everything I found is consistent with manual strangulation."

"Which is what we thought," Lawson said.

"Any surprises?" I asked.

"Yeah, a big one. It's not in his medical records, but this young man had one of his kidney's removed."

"Why is that a big surprise?" Lawson asked.

"Because," he said, "it was done very recently."

The pathologist hung up. Lawson searched through Allen's file. I waited.

"Allen hasn't been to an outside hospital the entire time he's been locked up," Lawson said when he came back on the line. "That mean what I think it does?"

"Either he was taken out secretly, unofficially . . . or it was removed inside."

"How the hell could an inmate have an organ removed inside the prison?"

I told him everything I knew about Alvarez and Baldwin, their shadowy pasts, their suspicious behavior, their involvement with Danny and Lance and Brent, and what I had learned about hypnosis.

"She can really make 'em stop bleeding and forget they were operated on?"

"It's possible."

"Why would they—"

"Why do people do most of the evil they do?" I said. "Money."

Something inside me jangled ever so slightly. Why? What was it? Money. Life insurance policies. Last will and testaments. Greed. Subterfuge. Black market organs.

Blackmail. That could be it. Money motive after all. Just not through life insurance. Private coercion and humiliation, not public. Private motives, not political ones.

"What about the scar?" he said.

"Baldwin probably gives them some explanation to believe while they're under that she and the doc reinforce when they're conscious again—tells them it's a cut or something. I don't know. I'm just guessing."

"I've got to notify the IG, FDLE, the—"

"Yes you do," I said.

"Then what?" he asked. "Do I try to detain them? Hold them 'til—"

"Don't tip them off. Just don't let them be alone with anyone. Make sure they can't cut on anyone else."

Juan Alvarez had arrived at the clinic he owned in Panama City shortly after six in the evening. No one had gone in or come out since then.

The front of the clinic, the waiting room and reception area, were dark, but lights burned in the back where the exam rooms were located.

Merrill and I were parked across the street in the lot of a closed insurance office. Waiting. Ironically, it was my inability to wait that had us here. Soon, several agencies, including FDLE, Potter and Bay County Sheriff Offices, and the Tallahassee and Panama City Police Departments would be investigating Alvarez and Baldwin, but that kind of bureaucratic cooperation took time, moved very slowly, and waiting for it could get more people hurt or killed.

We were close. I could feel it. We had momentum. Waiting would endanger more lives, and truthfully, selfishly,

I wanted to see this to the end.

If the other agencies showed up, Merrill and I would back away quietly. If they didn't, we'd try not to do anything to jeopardize the case they would eventually try to make.

"You really think they selling inmates' spare parts on eBay?" Merrill asked.

"I doubt they're using eBay."

"Wonder how long they been at it?"

"Haven't been at PCI long," I said. "Couldn't have done many. No telling what they did before they washed up there. People like them do damage everywhere they go."

He nodded. "Think they targeted the Kings or—"

"Probably start with inmates who spend a lot of time in Medical or Psychology, then narrow those down by blood type and ease of induction."

"Ease of what?"

"Their ability to be hypnotized."

Lights shone on the street, and a black Mercedes pulled in and parked near the side entrance of the clinic.

A young Hispanic man jumped out and ran inside.

"We crash the party now," Merrill said, "or wait until—"

Before he could finish his sentence, the young man rushed out of the clinic carrying an orange ice chest with red medical stickers that clashed with the cooler.

He jumped into his car and sped off.

We followed.

He led us out of the downtown district and across town on side streets, Merrill lying back, as often as possible keeping a few cars between us.

He was probably not expecting a tail, but even if he were, I doubt he could spot Merrill. In any event, he didn't seem to notice much of anything. He was too busy trying to look cool as he nodded his head to the beat. My guess was the only time he looked in the rearview mirror was to see himself.

Eventually, he led us to the airport.

He pulled into long-term parking and we followed. He got a time-and-date stamped ticket and so did we.

Merrill pulled in beside the Mercedes, putting my door next to the driver's. I waited until he was out of his car before I shoved my door into him.

The door struck him in the back and slammed him up against his car. But before I could get all the way out the door, he swung around and drew a gun from a shoulder holster and pointed it at me.

The sound of Merrill's .357 as he thumbed back the hammer and placed it just behind the guy's ear got his attention.

He lowered his gun and handed it to Merrill.

I climbed out of Merrill's truck and closed the door.

"What's your name?"

"Justo."

"Justo who?"

"Alvarez."

"How're you related to Juan?"

"He's my uncle. Sort of."

"What brings you to the airport tonight?"

"To visit relatives."

"Where?" Merrill asked.

"Miami," he said, cutting his eyes toward Merrill nervously, not daring to turn his head.

"Cool-looking suitcase you got there," I said, nodding toward the orange ice chest he was holding.

"It is a present for my mother."

"She need a transplant?"

His mouth actually fell open.

"What is it?"

He didn't say anything.

"Obvious he a brain donor," Merrill said.

"You do not understand. It is a special pie I made for her."

"You made your mother a pie?" Merrill said.

"Well, not me, but my aunt."

He was just saying the first thing that came to his mind, and as lame as it was, it was the story he was sticking to.

"She is very ill and I bring her what she loves when I visit her."

"That why it has medical stickers on it?" I asked.

He nodded. "*Sí.* Yes."

"Open it," Merrill said. "I like homemade pie."

"It will ruin it if I open the container."

Without moving the gun, Merrill used his other hand to grab the container and hand it to me.

I broke the medical seal with a key and opened it.

Inside was a human kidney on ice.

"I am trying to save a life," he said. "Please. I implore you."

"Well, hell," Merrill said, "why didn't you say so sooner. We didn't realize you were imploring us."

"Please."

"Tell us what the fuck's going on," Merrill said.

He shook his head.

"You rather tell the police?" I asked. "Tell us and you walk."

"Don't tell us," Merrill added, "you may never walk again."

He seemed to consider this a moment.

Eventually, Merrill hit him in the back of the neck with the butt of his gun.

"He harvests organs and sells them to wealthy people around the world. They go from here to Miami and then to Cuba or Mexico. Sometime other places."

"Who's giving up their organs?" I asked.

Merrill added, "And are they doing it willingly?"

"Inmates mainly," he said. "Sometimes women who come to his clinic for abortions. Can I go now?"

"He use Dr. Baldwin to hypnotize them?" I asked.

"The prison shrink lady? Yeah."

"For anesthesia? To make them forget?"

"Both, I believe . . . and . . . to stop the bleeding. Please. We're saving lives. No one is getting hurt."

"How you figure that?" Merrill said.

"We are stopping anyway. Uncle wants out. One more. That's it. Then no more."

"One more?" I asked.

"Si."

"After this one?"

"Si."

That's it, I thought. "I've got to call the institution." I pulled out my phone and punched in the number.

"Why he quittin'?" Merrill asked.

Justo shrugged.

"Danny and Brent dying," I said. "Too much heat."

"Don't think your ass ain't testifying against these sick fucks," Merrill said.

"You said I could go."

"No, *he* said you could walk. I said—"

Shots began to ring out, pocking metal, shattering glass all around us.

Merrill and I dove to the ground and rolled for cover. Justo fell to the ground after being shot twice in the chest. He was dead.

When the shots stopped we jumped up to see the Hispanic cowboy who had warned me off at the convenience store speeding out of the parking lot.

He yelled, "Hey amigo. I shot someone now, haven't I? Mother fuck."

Chapter Forty-four

I was racing back toward the institution in Merrill's truck.

He was at the airport awaiting the arrival of the cops.

"Sure," he'd said before I left, "leave the black man to deal with the po-lice. What could go wrong?"

On my way, I called Dad and had him call the sheriff of Bay County and ask him to personally respond to the scene to preclude the possibility of anything going wrong.

I then called the institution and asked the control room sergeant to find the inspector for me and to let me know if Alvarez or Baldwin try to reenter the prison.

"John, they're both already here," she said.

"Find the inspector," I said. "Have him call me as soon as possible."

When I reached the institution, I ran to the control room.

In the parking lot not far from Alvarez's and Baldwin's cars, I saw Hahn's. The way I had things figured, she wasn't involved in any of this. Was I wrong? Had she been playin' me all along?

"Inspector's not answering his phone."

"Keep trying. Tell him I'm in Medical. To get down

there as soon as he can."

The control room sergeant buzzed me in and I jogged down the dark compound and entered Medical.

The empty waiting room was dim, the hallways eerily quiet.

Mom is dead.

The unbidden thought rose out of the darkness and silence, and I was overcome by an oppressive sadness.

Pausing a moment, I leaned against the wall in the narrow hall, squinting against tears and trying to catch my breath.

The heaviness on my chest was severe, the hollowness inside cavernous, and I was separated from everything, even my own body, by a great dark distance.

Wasn't really until this moment that I realized the extent to which I was still in shock.

How is this possible? We weren't close. I was prepared. I dealt with death all the time.

I started laughing. It was all I could do in the face of such thoughts. I should know better, but I had been reduced by the great reducer, regressed by death.

"I want you to continue to focus and concentrate on that spot," Bailey Baldwin was saying to Lance Phillips, "and listen fully as I speak to you. As you focus on that spot, I'd like you to begin by just resting back in the way that's most comfortable for you."

Lance had been sitting up in an infirmary bed. Now, he was lying back on the stack of pillows.

"Good," Baldwin continued. "As you recline, you begin to notice the feelings and sensations in your body. Just notice some of them. For instance, as you continue staring at the spot, you may become aware of your feet, or you may become aware of the bed you're lying on, how soft it is, how comfortable. And as you do, you can pay attention to your breathing, and the sensations you experience with every breath you take."

I was standing near the open door of the infirmary, the dark hallway hiding my presence. From where I stood, I could see not only Baldwin hypnotizing Lance, but Alvarez preparing for surgery in the first exam room.

"As you continue concentrating on that spot, I'm going to begin to count. Each time I say an odd number, I'd like you to close your eyes. Each time I say an even number, I'd like you to open them and see that spot again. So, when I say *one*, you will close your eyes, and when I say *two*, you will open your eyes. Do you understand?"

Lance nodded very slowly.

"Close your eyes on each odd number and open them on each even number," she said. "And as you open and close your eyes, they will begin to become more and more tired and relaxed, until before long, they'll feel so tired that they'll simply remain closed. And then you will sink into a very peaceful hypnotic sleep.

"One. Two. Three. Allow your body to become more and more comfortable and at ease. Four. Become aware of that spot again. Five. Six. Seven. Your comfort is increasing. You are relaxing. Eight. Nine. Just let go. Ten. Eleven. Twelve. Now, your eyelids stick. You can't open them . . . It's okay. Be at peace. Perfect peace. Total rest. After this procedure, you'll never have felt so rested and so well in all your life."

The door to the exam room opened, and I ducked into the nurses' station.

Alvarez walked into the infirmary wearing green surgical scrubs, his thick black-and-gray hair covered by a sterile green head covering.

I pulled out my phone and began to record.

After a few moments, they rolled him out of the infirmary, down across the hall, and into the exam room.

I followed.

I recorded as they continued to make all the preparations, then snuck back into the nurses' station to call security. I didn't think handling Alvarez or Baldwin would be a problem, but it'd be nice to have more witnesses to what was going on.

I punched in the number for the control room.

The officer on duty answered on the second ring.

"Did y'all find the inspector?" I whispered.

"Hold on. Let me check with the sergeant," she said. "It's the chaplain. You find the inspector yet? Hold on, she's on the phone now. You still looking for Miss Ling? She's on her way out. I can—"

"Yeah. Let me speak to her."

"John?" Hahn said. "Where are you?"

"Brent Allen's grandfather was the motive," I said. "Find the OIC. I need backup in—"

Something bit me on the neck. I slapped at it, hitting a hard plastic object and a . . . what? Hand?

I spun around to see Alvarez standing there with a syringe.

I swung at him, but my knees buckled and I fell to the floor.

"What'd you give . . ." was all I could get out.

From the fallen receiver next to me on the floor I could hear Hahn, but I couldn't respond, couldn't . . .

Everything grew dim, distancing itself from me, as if I were sinking into a . . .

"**T**hey're criminals," Baldwin was saying. "You really think it's wrong to save an innocent person's life by taking an organ a criminal can live without?"

I tried to say something but was unable.

"He cannot respond," Alvarez said. "All he can do is breathe and blink."

"Well, we're saving lives and I want him to know. Innocent lives. People who deserve to live, who are doing good in the world, not killing and stealing and cheating and hurting their wives and abandoning their children like these poor excuses for human beings we're removing non-essential organs from."

The two thieves hovered over me, their faces floating in and out of view.

I was lying on one of the infirmary beds, unable to do anything but breathe and blink, wondering if the death that seemed to always surround me was about to lay claim to me.

"This gives us the second kidney we were looking for," Alvarez said.

"*His?*" she asked, nodding toward me, eyes wide. "I don't have time to put him under and—"

"There is no need. We are leaving."

"Well, be quick."

He drifted away from view and I wondered if he was already slicing me open.

"He's looking at us," Baldwin said. "Can't you put him to sleep?"

I didn't hear him answer, but within another few moments, unconsciousness rolled in on me. I fought to stay awake, to keep my eyes open, but . . .

Chapter Forty-five

When I woke up, I was lying on a bed in the infirmary, Merrill looking down at me.

I tried to sit up, but only got part of the way. In the process, I noticed a needle in my arm.

"IV," he said. "They pumpin' out the shit Alvarez put in you."

"Where is . . ."

"In custody. Lawson's with them in the security building, making the handoff to your dad. He'll hold them for FDLE. Both kept sayin' they ain't killed nobody and can prove it."

"Hahn?"

"She the one brought backup down here. Saying something about Allen's granddad. Told Lawson you'd explain everything when you woke up. She took Phillips back to the quad. Down there checking him out now."

I tried to get up again, and again I got about halfway up and fell back down.

"Help me up."

"Just tell me what to do. You stay—"

"We gotta get down there."

He pulled me up as I snatched out the IV. The nurse ran in, but we waved her away.

"Tell me Hahn ain't involved in this," he said.

I stepped and stumbled and he half carried me through Medical, out into the night, and through the center gate toward the lower compound.

My hands were tingling, my whole body stiff and weak, not responding the way I wanted it to.

"Did Hahn help the docs kill Jacobs and Allen?"

I shook my head, still finding it difficult to talk. "They didn't . . . Why this was the last one."

"Hell, I usually can't follow you when you able to talk . . . so this'll be . . ."

I said, "What . . . would their . . . motive be . . . for trying to kill Lance?"

"Cover-up."

"*Before* . . . they operated . . . on him? They took organs . . . from inmates . . . didn't kill . . . them. When Allen was killed, the autopsy revealed what they had been doing."

"Not that, who tryin' to kill Phillips?"

"Allen was the real target all along."

"Got to be Emile Rollins then. Only one left."

Even with his help, I was moving slowly. The best I could do was small shutter steps like an inmate in shackles.

"First attempt on Lance was in a confinement cell. Emile couldn't've done that."

"Got to be staff. Baldwin? Alvarez? Foster?"

"Only one person . . . could've done it," I said.

I could feel myself waking up, the stiffness in my muscles breaking up and dissipating, the fogginess in my brain clearing, my vocal chords loosening, but my head throbbed and my vision was blurry.

"Who?"

I took in a breath.

"Lance himself. His cell door . . . was never unlocked. No one drugged him or . . . hypnotized him. Danny brought him the rope, but he did it to himself. It was smart. Make himself look like the intended victim from the very beginning. It was convincing too. In fact, I think he pushed it a little too far and nearly killed himself. If the nurse hadn't gotten in the cell in time . . . He continued to play the victim and deflect suspicion by hiring the inmates to stage the attack on him in the chapel."

"So he killed . . ."

"Danny and Brent. Switched bunks with them, made up that shit about his mattress being more comfortable and Danny feeling safer up there to make it look like their deaths were really attempts on him. This whole thing was never about an attempt on Lance or the actual murder of Danny. Those were attempts to disguise the real motive for the murder of Brent Allen."

"Which was?"

"Money. The motive for all this elaborate deception, and the taking of life, is money. It is all about greed."

Up ahead the dorms rose up out of the darkness, floodlights illuminating their bulky, blocky gray masses.

"That why he used the cards?" he asked. "Make sure everybody know it was murder and not suicide so insurance company would pay?"

I shook my thick head slowly. "Nothing to do with that. He used the cards so he could make himself look like a victim. It was never about the life insurance. The Suicide Kings was something he used for subterfuge."

"Thought you said it was about—"

"Money, yeah. The small fortune left to Brent Allen by his grandfather. The life insurance scheme was just a cover for the real motive. The coverage had already lapsed. What he wanted was to be in Allen's will, not the beneficiary of the policy. He's about to get out. Allen's grandfather just died. He will inherit. A lot."

Merrill shook his head.

"I think maybe he talked Danny into attempting or pretending to attempt to hang himself since he had just done it in Confinement, and then he made sure it really worked—or maybe he didn't care. Just wanted it to look like another attempt. But with Brent . . . he couldn't take any chances. He traded bunks with him, strangled him, then let him lie on the floor beside his bunk before he hung him. He's the only one who could've. He was right under him."

"So Baldwin and Alvarez . . ."

"Didn't have anything to do with the murders," I said. "In fact, they were the last thing they wanted. They got caught because one of their victims, Allen, was also Lance's. They didn't kill their victims—that brings autopsies and investigations. They just stole their organs."

"You think he knows you know?"

I nodded. "He didn't stick around Medical—and Hahn to take him back. I think she might be—"

"Think you can move your slow ass any faster, or I gotta carry you?"

"I'm starting to come out of it."

"Then quit doin' the inmate shuffle and get you ass in gear."

Chapter Forty-six

We were buzzed in to the massive hangar-like structure of D-dorm, then into Quad-3 to find Hahn standing on the top rail of the second-story catwalk, a noose tied around her neck.

Lance stood just behind her.

Made of several sheets tied together, the noose was looped through a metal support beam in the high ceiling. The beam worked as a pulley. Every time Lance pulled down on the noose, it pulled up on Hahn's neck.

Her hands were tied at her sides with an inmate belt, the tips of her shoes barely touching the top bar of the railing.

Face puffy and pale, eyes bulging, little helpless, fearful whimpers escaped from her constricted airway, out of her tight mouth, and into the enormous open space of the concrete-and-steel enclosure.

To our left, the empty metal staircase leading to the upper rows of cell doors and the cement catwalk provided a clear path to Hahn, but it was too tall, would take too long to climb. She would be dead before we could get to her.

Below the walkway, the solid steel cell doors in front of us were closed, dark behind their small strip of glass.

"Don't come any closer," Lance yelled.

The quad was so large, its ceiling so high, his words were quickly lost in that airy, white-noise sound of the huge space.

He yanked on the sheet wrapped around his arms and it snatched Hahn up, her shoes slipping off her feet and falling down to the bare concrete floor below, taking a moment to reach the floor because of the distance, bouncing as they smacked the cement, the loud sound of their crash ricocheting off the hard surfaces.

Hahn gasped, the pitch of her whimpers becoming more shrill, more childlike, more panicked.

Most of the men had been in their cells, many of them sleeping, but a small group was beginning to gather on the ground floor. They looked up in silence, obviously shocked at what they were seeing.

"Get them outta here," Merrill said.

A CO had just rushed in from the officers' station, but was too busy looking up wide-eyed at Hahn to respond.

"Now."

He began to slowly herd the resistant inmates. Merrill turned and took a few steps toward them and they began to move much faster.

Within a few moments we were alone with Lance and Hahn in the quad.

If he didn't release some of the tension in the sheets soon, there would just be three of us.

"Ease off on the pressure some," I yelled up at him. "Lower her down just a little. Please."

"Why should I?"

"What do you want? Why're you doing this?"

"My whole life . . . nothin' ever works out for me. Everybody's always . . . everything's been against me. I'm . . ."

"You're a very rich man now," I said. "The world is a different place for someone with the kind of money you have."

He cocked his head and seemed to think about it. Looking down at me, he said, "But they'll never give me the money now."

"It's yours. Nothing anyone can do. Oh, they may try to get it back, but you can hire the best lawyers."

"Hell," Merrill said, "you can OJ all this shit away. Beat the charges. Live the good life on the golf course every day. All it takes is money."

"If you let Hahn go," I said. "You can't kill her in front of us, with us standing here watching, and expect . . ."

He fed a little slack to the noose.

Hahn's feet touched the rail again and some of the color began to come back into her face.

"The response team will be here any minute. Place'll be full of officers with guns. Let her go now. Let us take you in. We can protect you. You know I will."

The PCI riot squad was a group of trigger-happy adrenaline junkies with far more testosterone than judgement. Its members were correctional officers who were good shots and gung-ho, all of whom had the required ego and requisite sophomoric swagger. We had to resolve this before they stormed the quad.

"I let go, she hangs," Lance said. "She'll fall and snap her neck. They shoot me, she dies."

"Don't let that happen. Go ahead and let her down."

"It took you a while," he said. "I almost fooled you, didn't I?"

"You did."

"I'm smarter than people think."

"You are."

As we spoke, Merrill slowly eased under the

overhang of the second-story walkway and over toward the stairs.

"If you could've just made them look like suicides and not used the cards . . ."

"But I had to look like a victim. I knew I'd be suspected as soon as people found out about Brent's will."

"Hiring the inmates to attack us in the chapel was a nice touch."

"You like that? I thought so too. I told 'em the most they could be charged with was assault and I'd make them rich for it. I knew they'd talk eventually, but I'd be long gone by then. Some warm tropical place without extradition, sipping champagne and earning interest. Fuckin' doctors fucked it up for me."

"It was a great plan. Ingenious. I mean really, really smart. I think you could get a book deal out of it."

He seemed to think about that, but only for a moment.

His head exploded a split second before the deafeningly loud report rang around the enormous concrete-and-steel box.

The riot squad ran in.

Boots on concrete.

Barking orders.

Radios blaring.

As Lance fell, he released his hold on the noose.

The sudden release of tension made Hahn lose her balance.

She tried to get it back, but couldn't and fell off the rail.

She didn't fall far.

The slack snapped out of the sheets, the noose tightening around her neck.

From the moment the shot was fired, Merrill was

running up the stairs.

I tried to get beneath Hahn to catch her, but she didn't fall far enough. Not even close. She was some two stories above me. Dangling. Dying.

When Merrill reached the place where Hahn had been a moment before and where Lance now lay dead, he couldn't reach the rope. Hahn was hanging from the high ceiling, the noose caught in the beams, too far away from the balcony for him to reach.

"What the fuck do I do?" he yelled. "I can't reach her."

I didn't have an answer.

The riot squad was yelling "CLEAR" and other congratulatory exclamations, seemingly oblivious to Hahn. They probably thought it was another inmate.

I spun around looking for something we could use to reach out from the balcony and pull the sheet rope in so we could grab her, but there was nothing. Anything that could've worked could've also been used as a weapon and wouldn't be in an inmate dorm.

Hahn was hanging above me and there was nothing I could do about it.

She had kicked a bit at first, but now the only movement was coming from the slight sway of the sheets, the only sound the small, sad creak that accompanied it.

"Why the fuck you shoot him?" Merrill yelled.

No one had an answer for that.

Someone yelled, "Get a ladder from maintenance down here. Now."

It would take too long, do Hahn no good.

Helpless.

Powerless.

Frustration and futility.

Unable to do anything else, I stood beneath Hahn,

looking up at her.

And I stayed that way. Long after anything could be done, long after she was dead, I still stood there, being with her mortal remains, being with my guilt.

I had been unable to save her, unable to prevent her death. I had failed her.

Now all I could do was stand, stay here with her as long as what was left of her was here. All I could do was be present, bear witness, watch over, grieve, and feel guilty.

Chapter Forty-seven

"He was killed over money?" Cheryl Jacobs said. "Not even—but to cover up the fact that someone else was being killed for money."

I frowned and nodded.

We were standing under the gazebo extending out over St. Joseph's Bay. I had just told her all I knew and guessed about her son's death.

"How do I live with that?"

"I'm not sure."

It was day's end, and beyond the bay, the entire, expansive horizon glowed a vibrant coral beneath a clear blue sky, both of which reflected on the gently bobbing surface of the bay waters below.

I thought about Hahn.

"There're things I can't live with," I said, "but I do."

She turned to me, her hurting, glistening eyes penetrating. "You ever lost a child?"

I shook my head. She was right. What did I know?

We were quiet for a long moment, the breeze coming in off the bay stinging our eyes, but not enough to account for the volume of water they were producing.

I had been unable to do anything for Hahn. I was unable to do anything for Cheryl. Except maybe just to be with her, silently suffering alongside her. Wasn't much, but it was something.

"This is all so fucked," she said.

I nodded. "Yes it is."

We stood there long after the glow of the horizon turned from coral to salmon to apricot to the charcoal gray of dusk.

Before us now the bay was growing black, a glass darkly reflecting the lights of the small town on either side of us.

I would stand with her for as long as she wanted, this childless mother, this stricken, inconsolable woman, weeping with those who weep, mourning with those who mourn, grieving with those who grieve.

I was sad.

For Cheryl. For Hahn. For my mom. For myself.

It was a little later that evening, dusk edging into darkness, and I was sitting in an uncomfortable wooden chair down by the river behind my trailer.

Thinking. Feeling. Processing.

No bottle. Nobody. Just me and my mind—my sometime enemy, sometime friend.

Guilt.

I could've saved Hahn. Should have.

I had been too distracted, too divided, too scattered. Between my new relationship with Anna, dealing with Mom's dying and death, the murder at Potter Farm, the Suicide Kings, the warden wanting my job, and Andy Bearden's body being found in the woods, I had not focused to the extent I should have.

I wasn't blaming anything I had going on—only my

approach, only my management.

I had been given enough time to keep Hahn from dying, but I had failed.

I had been given the grace of time to repair my relationship with my mom but I had not taken full advantage of it, had done only part of the work.

I had not devoted enough time and energy to finding out who killed the young woman propped up on the prison fence and had barely begun to investigate what really happened to Andy Bearden.

Well, I could do it now.

With nothing left to do in the Suicide Kings case, I could put aside my mourning for my mom for the moment and concentrate completely on the Potter Farm victim.

Sitting up and taking three deep breaths and letting each one out slowly, I opened more than just my mind to what I knew and what I didn't know.

I had something earlier, when I got the little jangling inside about real motive for Brent Allen's murder. Something. What was it? Money. Life insurance policies. Last will and testaments. Greed. Subterfuge. Black market organs. Blackmail. Money motive. Blackmail. That was it. Private blackmail. Private humiliation and coercion, not public, not political. Private.

Why was she at the farm that night? What was her real motive for being there?

Had she really not gone into the house?

Who had killed her? Why? Why stage her body against the fence at the prison? Why steal her body? Had the killer stolen the body? Was it even related? I thought about when it had happened and where. I thought again about what the driver had said.

What secret did her body hold? Why take the risk of stealing her like that?

I thought about Judge Cox's crazy proclamation that it was part of the gay agenda and Don Stockton saying everything ultimately came back to the money motive. Ralph Long was in the closet. He was also as motivated by money as anyone I knew.

Names. Faces. Andrew Sullivan. Chris Taunton. Deacon Jones. Hugh Glenn. Donnie Foster. Dad.

Hugh wanted to embarrass Dad. Who else wanted to embarrass any of the other candidates?

I thought about possible motives for murder. Money. Greed. Jealousy. Rage. Revenge. Sociopathy. Power. To silence. To cover another crime. To—

That was it.

The right key inserted, the pins aligned in the tumbler, rotation of the plug, and everything began to fall into place.

Unlocked. Opened.

Chapter Forty-eight

"**Y**ou had sex with the victim at the farm that night," I said.

He started to deny it.

"I'm just telling you what I think," I said. "But if I'm right, there's evidence to back up everything I say."

Somehow without acknowledging or agreeing with anything I'd said so far, he indicated for me to go on.

"You had a little more to drink than you normally do," I said.

"I shouldn't've had anything," he said. "I rarely ever do."

It wasn't late but it was dark outside and seemed later than it was. We were in Judge Richard Cox's home office. Just the two of us, in an otherwise very still, very quiet house.

"But you did drink and your inhibitions were down. Melanie Sagal told me what you like, what you want to do that your wife won't do. And the blonde, who never went inside—Carla Jean said she never let anyone in—came on to you in the parking area, near your car, after most everyone was gone."

He nodded.

"Offered to give you what you wanted," I said.

"Said she had always been attracted to me, to my wisdom and the way I used my power. Said she wanted nothin' more in the world than for me to fuck her in the ass. She was so assertive, so in charge, and I was so turned on."

"So y'all got in your big black car and had anal sex."

"The best sex of my life," he said. "I've never . . . it was . . . so good."

"And when you were done . . . there was a revelation," I said. "Did you make the discovery or—"

"No," he said. "I was still . . . enraptured."

"The reveal came because the whole encounter was a setup."

He nodded.

"You had just had sex—according to you, the best sex of your life—with a man."

"I didn't believe her at first," he said. "See, I still call her a *her*. She actually had to pull her panties aside and show me her penis before I'd believe her."

"Someone had decided to teach you a lesson," I said. "To make you question your sexual assumptions and your homophobic rhetoric."

He nodded. "She said as much."

"Which is why you proclaimed this to be a part of a gay agenda at the debate the other night."

He nodded again.

"And when she showed you her penis?" I asked. "When you looked down there and saw it lying there right above where you had just been . . ."

"I lost it," he said. "I hit her. I'm old and not very

strong, but I was on top of him and I used my weight to hold him there and I hit him. And hit him. And hit him."

"But you didn't kill him," I said. "You're old and weak and were tired and drunk and spent. The most you did was daze him a little."

"I didn't kill anybody," he said. "I couldn't. But how do you know?"

"After you went inside to call your daughter and wait for her to pick you up—something you did because you were too shaken up to drive, not because you thought you had too much to drink—a witness saw her stumbling toward the barn. You didn't kill her because she was beaten to death and because she had run—actually, been chased for a long way right before she was murdered, and she fought too, put up a hell of a struggle, which is why rigor mortis set in as fast as it did and the killer was able to prop her up against the prison fence."

"But why do that?" he asked. "Why take her to the prison? Why prop her up?"

"He chased her through the woods between Potter Farm and the prison," I said. "Probably killed her somewhere near where the woods end on the other side. Saw the prison. Thought it would be a way to remove suspicion from the farm."

"I couldn't believe it when I heard where she was," he said.

"And you panicked," I said. "You thought if the ME did an autopsy he'd see she was really a guy dressed as a girl and eventually the whole world would know that the anti-gay 'marriage is between one man and one woman' judge had had sex with a man."

He nodded.

"So you grabbed a Halloween mask and a shotgun and followed the funeral home hearse on the way to the morgue, ran him off the road, and stole the body. You then drove to the first dirt road you came to, raced down it until you saw the trailer—"

"I saw a tree stand first, but when I got out I saw the trailer and . . ."

"You carried him into the trailer, took all the clothes and makeup and jewelry and wig off of him, then shot a dead man in the head with the shotgun to try to cover up the beating he had taken, the other wounds, and his identity."

"I did. I did all that, but I didn't kill him. I wouldn't. I couldn't. So who did?"

"Think about the motive," I said. "You thought it was a gay agenda."

"Yeah?"

"It was an agenda, but a personal not a public one."

"Huh?"

"Richie," I said. "This was about a son sick of hearing his dad condemn him every time he opened his mouth. He wanted to—"

"Show you how ignorant you were," Richie said, stepping into the room. "How wrong you were about us, about me. I thought if you had sex with Andy you'd understand."

"Andy?"

"The guy you fucked, Dad," he said. "He's—was a friend of mine. He was in my last play. We hung out."

"Why'd you kill him?" his dad asked.

"He had an agenda of his own," Richie said. "He

wasn't just doin' it for me. He threatened to go public, to make sure you didn't get reelected, to expose the hypocrisy of politicians like you. He recorded you. He was gonna post it on Youtube. Share it with the whole world. Make a mockery of you."

"So you killed him?"

"I tried to talk to him."

"When?"

"While Diane was driving you home. Remember, I followed y'all with your car. 'Cept I didn't follow right away. I tried to talk some sense into Andy. I found him down by the lake washing his face. He wouldn't listen so then I tried to get his phone from him so I could destroy the evidence against you, but he ran . . . and I chased him. We fought. I didn't mean to kill him. I just . . . I was tryin' to protect my dad."

"Your dad?" I said. "Or you dad's job and the money he's paid to do it, the money he gives you. See, I think you let your real motive slip at the community center the night of the debate. What was it Diane told you? Try living without the assistance he gives y'all. I think you did it for money, which means if your dad does get reelected, every dime he ever makes will be blood money."

Richie reached behind his back and came out with a gun—a small .38 revolver popular for personal protection, the kind I was certain his dad had a carry permit for.

"He *is* gonna be reelected, because no one's ever gonna know what happened," he said.

He pointed the gun at me.

"*Richie*," Judge Cox said.

"I can't let you do this to us, John," Richie said, ignoring his Dad. "I'm sorry. I like you."

"You liked Andy too, didn't you?" I said. "So we know that doesn't carry any weight with you."

"*Richie,*" his dad said again. "Put the gun down. Now."

"I've got to do this, Dad. For you. For us. This whole mess is my fault. I can't let our family fall for some stupid prank I tried to pull on you."

"Richie," I said, "I'm wearing a wire. Everything that has been said is being recorded by my dad's department. They'll be in here as soon as I give the signal. You've got no play. Don't make things worse."

"What's the signal?" he said. "Wait. Don't say it. Show me the wire. I want to see it. I don't believe you."

Before I could show him, Dad, Jake, and another couple of deputies entered the room, guns drawn.

"It's over, Richie," Dad said. "Put the gun down."

He nodded. And for a minute he looked like he was actually going to do it. But then, in a split second, in far less time than it takes to tell it, he brought the gun up to his temple and pulled the trigger.

His dad screamed.

Diane ran into the room.

Dad and the other deputies rushed him.

But there was no use. We were the unwitting witnesses of a successful suicide.

Chapter Forty-nine

All the way home I tried to reach Anna, but each time I called, her phone went straight to voicemail.

My heart was heavy. More for Hahn than anyone else at the moment. But I felt bad for the Cox family too.

I was beyond exhausted, rawbone weary, utterly depleted, finding even the effortless act of driving too much.

I had the urge to drop by Mom's and check on her but it was too late. And then I realized the real reason I couldn't—and just how too late it really was.

That made me feel even more disconnected, distant even from myself.

My senses were overwhelmed, overloaded with loss and violence and death.

I continued to try Anna, and continued to get her voicemail.

When I reached our solitary trailer in the second phase of the Prairie Palm Mobile Home Community, I knew why.

The lights were on inside and out, the front door flung open wide.

Chris Taunton's car was beside Anna's in the yard.

I parked and rushed in.

The place was trashed, obvious signs of struggle everywhere I looked.

It didn't take long to search the small trailer.

Anna wasn't here. Neither was Chris.

Had he taken her? If he had, it hadn't been far. Not without one of their cars. Was he attacking her right now? Were they outside?

I ran out the back door, searching the backyard, down toward the river.

There was no sign they had been out here.

The same was true of the front and side yards and nearly a mile in every direction.

I searched both their vehicles, including their trunks, but they weren't there either.

As I neared the trailer again, a deep sense of dread began to set in.

Where could she be? What had happened? Had she been taken? If so, why?

Did Chris have something to do with it? If so, why would he leave his car? Even if he had someone else helping him in another vehicle, why would he leave his car here?

Was it possible Chris had nothing to do with it? Was he as much a victim as Anna was? Did he show up at the wrong time? If so, why take him too?

It didn't make sense. None of it did. But it would. It all would. And I wouldn't stop until it did.

My phone rang. I didn't recognize the number.

"John Jordan," I said.

"I have your wife," he said.

I didn't recognize the voice. It wasn't Chris.

"She is safe. She is fine. But if you contact the

authorities she is dead. If you tell anyone—anyone at all—
she is dead. If you do not do exactly what I say when I say,
she is dead."

I didn't say anything.

"Do you understand?" he asked.

"I do."

"Thank you for not making ridiculous threats and
absurd proclamations. You are wise. This is going to run
very smoothly. You do what I say when I say and you'll
have her back safe and sound very soon."

"Can I speak to her?"

"When I call back," he said. "When I have her
situated. For now I just wanted to make sure you didn't
contact anyone before you knew exactly what was going
on."

"I won't call anyone," I said.

"I have her ex-husband too. He came up as we were
leaving and tried to be a hero. He will turn up dead in the
next day or so. It will appear to be an accident. You will
know what I am capable of."

"I only care about Anna," I said. "Do what you want
to with Chris, but there's no need to kill him to convince
me of anything. I'm convinced."

I wasn't sure if that was enough to save Chris's life,
but I wasn't sure there was much more I could do.

"I'll do anything to get her back," I said.

"That's what I'm counting on."

There was so much more I wanted to say, but I knew
better.

"I'll call back soon," he said. "Be ready."

About the Author

Multi-award-winning novelist Michael Lister is a native Floridian best known for literary suspense thrillers and mysteries.

The Florida Book Review says that "Vintage Michael Lister is poetic prose, exquisitely set scenes, characters who are damaged and faulty," and Michael Koryta says, "If you like crime writing with depth, suspense, and sterling prose, you should be reading Michael Lister," while Publisher's Weekly adds, "Lister's hard-edged prose ranks with the best of contemporary noir fiction."

Michael grew up in North Florida near the Gulf of Mexico and the Apalachicola River in a small town world famous for tupelo honey.

Truly a regional writer, North Florida is his beat.

In the early 90s, Michael became the youngest chaplain within the Florida Department of Corrections. For nearly a decade, he served as a contract, staff, then senior chaplain at three different facilities in the Panhandle of Florida—a unique experience that led to his first novel, 1997's critically acclaimed, POWER IN THE BLOOD. It was the first in a series of popular and celebrated novels featuring ex-cop turned prison chaplain, John Jordan. Of the John Jordan series, Michael Connelly says, "Michael Lister may be the author of the most unique series running in mystery fiction. It crackles with tension and authenticity," while Julia Spencer-Fleming adds, "Michael Lister writes one of the most ambitious and unusual crime fiction series going. See what crime fiction is capable of."

Michael also writes historical hard-boiled thrillers, such as THE BIG GOODBYE, THE BIG BEYOND, and THE BIG HELLO featuring Jimmy "Soldier" Riley, a PI in Panama City during World War II (www.SoldierMysteries.com). Ace Atkins calls the "Soldier" series "tough and violent with snappy dialogue and great atmosphere . . . a suspenseful, romantic and historic ride."

Michael Lister won his first Florida Book Award for his literary novel DOUBLE EXPOSURE. His second Florida Book Award was for his fifth John Jordan novel BLOOD SACRIFICE.

Michael also writes popular and highly praised columns on film and art and meaning and life that can be found at www.WrittenWordsRemain.com.

His nonfiction books include the "Meaning" series: THE MEANING OF LIFE, MEANING EVERY MOMENT, and THE MEANING OF LIFE IN MOVIES.

Lister's latest literary thrillers include DOUBLE EXPOSURE, THUNDER BEACH, BURNT OFFERINGS, SEPARATION ANXIETY, and A CERTAIN RETRIBUTION.

Thank you for reading BLOOD MONEY!

And don't miss BLOOD MOON to find out what happens next.

Be sure to visit www.MichaelLister.com for more about other John Jordan Mysteries and Michael's other exciting novels.

Sign up for Michael's Monthly Newsletter at www.MichaelLister.com to receive news, updates, special offers, and another book absolutely FREE!

CPSIA information can be obtained at www.ICGtesting.com
Printed in the USA
LVOW11*1450101115

461886LV00007B/54/P